"Here I am, right on track. Or was, until..."

"Until you met me."

She nodded, but something about the familiar intimacy in his voice, the hint of remembered laughter, made her smile.

"So your first instinct was to make a new plan. You need it."

"I...I do," she admitted. "It seemed the only way to make sense of this whole situation. But seeing it through your eyes, it's clear I need it a little too much, that there are times when going with the flow or being more flexible can have their place. But it's not something I can just turn off. And trust me, I've never felt more like I need a plan than I have this week."

"So we'll work something out together." His voice sounded rough, low, and she looked up to catch the concern on his face, mixed with a distance she hadn't felt from him before. He shook his head, and when he looked back at her his expression was lighter, sunnier.

"When do we start?"

He laughed and leaned back on his arms, one of them nudging slightly behind her back. "How about not right this minute? If we say we'll make a start today, is that enough of a plan for now?"

"It'll do." She grinned.

Dear Reader,

Some of you might recognize Rachel, the heroine of *Bound by a Baby Bump*. She started life as a minor character in another story, but I was so captivated by her that I decided she needed a book of her own.

I knew from the start that Rachel was the consummate organizer—always together, always in control—and so it seemed clear what she needed to shake up her life: a baby! From there I had the enviable job of crafting a hero who would challenge her, push her and make her face her past. Leo, with his commitment to chaos, is just the man.

It was a pleasure watching these characters grow together, facing their past and creating a family, and I hope that you enjoy their journey as much as I have.

Best wishes,

Ellie Darkins

Bound by a Baby Bump

Ellie Darkins

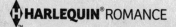

HARLEQUIN® ROMANCE

Recycling programs
for this product may
not exist in your area.

ISBN-13: 978-0-373-74339-1

Bound by a Baby Bump

First North American Publication 2015

Copyright © 2015 by Ellie Darkins

Printed in U.S.A.

Ellie Darkins spent her formative years devouring romance novels, and after completing her English degree she decided to make a living from her love of books. As a writer and editor her work now entails dreaming up romantic proposals, hot dates with alpha males and trips to the past with dashing heroes. When she's not working she can usually be found at her local library or out for a run.

Also by Ellie Darkins

HARLEQUIN ROMANCE

Frozen Heart, Melting Kiss

Visit the Author Profile page
at Harlequin.com for more titles.

For my family

CHAPTER ONE

Look up.

He commanded her to feel his gaze on her skin, to glance over and meet his eye. To make a connection with him. He'd been watching her for hours, biding his time until he could have her complete, undivided attention. Since the moment he'd first seen her striding round the room, her tablet computer and Bluetooth headset at odds with her black silk evening dress and staggeringly sexy heels, he'd been transfixed.

The curve of her calves, the gleam of her skin and the fluid movement of her hair had caught his attention, but it was her fierce concentration that had held it. The way she'd managed the room and everyone in it with a gentle nudge here and a subtle pull there. With a glance at her watch and a whisper in the ear of a member of staff she'd averted disasters, negotiated tricky situations and ensured that every person she spoke to ended their conversation with a beaming grin. No doubt the charity the gala was fundraising for would make a fortune.

Under normal circumstances, the thought of a to-do list and a watch filled his belly with apprehension, an unwelcome reminder of school days that had tormented him at the time, and still threatened the occasional nightmare more than ten years later. But worn as an accessory by a woman who seemed so effortlessly powerful, it was suddenly incredibly sexy.

He'd waited for the perfect moment all night—watching groups where she was conversing, catching her eye across the room; at one point, he'd even headed towards her with a determined stride—only for her to abruptly change course and disappear into the kitchen. And now she was putting her head together with one of the other guests, consulting her tablet, tucking a curtain of shining hair behind her ear.

She laughed, and the sound reached him as clear as if the room had been silent. Her face creased, her head dropped back, and humour radiated from her like a wave. He wanted to make her laugh. He was unreasonably jealous of the person who had inspired the sound, a man with pure silver hair and a walking stick.

The string band had started playing in a corner of the ballroom, and a few couples were heading towards the dance floor. His eyes flickered towards them, and he wondered whether she'd accept an invitation to dance.

In the moment that his eyes left her, he felt her look at him.

He whipped around to try and catch her gaze, but her eyes had already dropped to her tablet, as she scrolled up and down. She glanced at him again, and this time he caught it. He turned, his hands in his pockets, and his body relaxed under her stare, turning his stance into something languid and louche.

He walked towards her, smiling, still refusing to look away. He would hold this contact until he could get his hands on something more solid.

Just a couple of steps away from her, he was hit with unaccustomed nerves. It had been an age since he'd felt nervous talking to a woman. Things were pretty easy-come-easy-go in his love-life, much to the satisfaction of everyone involved. Nerves were thin on the ground when the most you were looking to gain or lose was a few nights or weeks of fun. The prospect of commitment, of expectations, of being caught in a situation with no simple way out—

only the fix of her eyes on his kept a shiver from his spine.

'Hi, I'm Rachel Archer.' The words arrived in a rush as soon as he was within arm's reach and she stuck out her hand for him to shake.

'Leo.' He just managed the one word, though it felt as if all breath had left his body at the feel of her hand in his. He observed her closely, looking for any clue that she was as affected by this meeting as he. But she had dropped her eyes, pulling her hand back—was that a fraction of a hesitation?—and glancing down at her tablet.

'So, are you enjoying crashing the party?' She gave a throaty chuckle with the words, and he absorbed the sound, revelling in the delicious heat it inspired in his body. He was so focused on that sound that he almost missed the meaning of her words.

'Crashing?' he asked with a raised eyebrow and a smile. 'Says who?'

'Says me.' No laugh this time, though a perfectly polite smile was still on her lips. He wanted a real one. 'Tonight is strictly invitation only, though if you are here to contribute *generously* to the Julia House hospice, I'm sure we can make an exception.'

He returned his hands to his pockets; it was on the tip of his tongue to tell her that he was there in place of his father, who was unwell and couldn't attend. Normally, 'representing the family' wasn't something he was interested in, but his father had promised the organisers that the family would be there with a generous donation—for a good cause he had been known to make an exception. He was intrigued, though. How did she know he was crashing—had she been asking questions about him?

'I want to know more about why you think I'm crashing.'

'Well…' she said, pulling up another page on her tablet. 'I planned the guest list. I sent the invitations, checked the RSVPs and wrote the table plan. There wasn't a single Leo to be seen.' Her eyes left her screen, and she looked him up and down, her eyes travelling from his face to his shoes, faltering slightly at his belt and chest. Encouraging.

'Ah, so I must be crashing. I take it your lists are never wrong?'

'Never,' she agreed with a good-tempered nod, and just the merest hint of another chuckle.

'Then I suppose I've got some making up to do. What will it take?'

'Well, apart from your considerable contribution to Julia House, which I'm sure is already in hand...'

'Naturally.'

'I want an explanation.'

It was his turn to laugh. 'That's all?' But she didn't look equally amused. In fact a worry line had appeared between her brows, and she glanced again at her screen.

'Tonight has been planned and re-planned, checked and double-checked. I want to know how you're here, and how I didn't know about it.'

He wanted that line gone. Wanted any evidence of discomfort wiped from her face. He still wanted to make her laugh.

'I'll tell you everything. Every dark secret and trick of the conman's trade.' He raised his eyebrows, attempting melodramatic villainy, and was rewarded with a lift at the corner of her lips. 'All you have to do is dance with me.'

Rachel rested her hand stiffly on his shoulder as they started to move to the music, wondering—again—why she had agreed to this. She let her gaze travel up from his collar, over a tanned throat, blond stubbled jaw and endearingly crooked nose. Up to a pair of eyes as blue as a baking summer sky, and then remembered.

Somewhere along the line, somewhere between guest list and dessert, her system had fallen short. He was probably standing in for someone—she had a shortlist of faces she'd been expecting to see but hadn't. But how had she made it to eleven o'clock without realising something was wrong?

'So,' she prompted, trying to keep her mind on the job, rather than on the confident way Leo was leading her around the floor, or the scent coming from his skin. Something salty, natural and that had, she guessed, never been anywhere near a Selfridges counter.

She faltered for a second as she caught him looking at her, and felt her cheeks warming under the intensity of his interest. She stilled, suddenly hyperaware of the pressure of his hand around hers, of his arm at her waist, the sound of him breathing close to her ear. Only the subtle squeeze of his arm reminded her she was supposed to be dancing. Forcing her feet to move, she glanced over his shoulder and spotted her boss, Will, and for a moment she was worried she was about to be caught slacking. But one look at his face told her she had nothing to worry about. He had eyes only for Maya, his partner, and she smiled. She couldn't help but take a little credit for the happiness that was radiating from them both. She was the one who'd engineered Will into taking a cookery course he wasn't interested in, all because it was run by a woman he definitely was.

She'd watched that relationship blossom, from first meeting to their elation tonight, and felt a little pang of…what? Loneliness? No, that wasn't it. She had friends—she'd even shared a flat with her best friend, Laura, until she'd bought her own place a year ago—right on track for her five-year plan. Sometimes she even managed to schedule time for a date or two.

But she didn't have *that*, whatever it was that made it look as if half the light in the room were emanating from them.

So no, she wasn't lonely, but maybe she was curious. Intrigued enough by the possibilities that when the surfy-looking blond who'd been casting looks in her direction all night had asked her if she wanted to dance, she'd looked him up and down and considered it.

And she'd been intrigued enough by what she'd seen to fight down the urge to tell him that this wasn't in her schedule, but to send him a smile instead.

There wasn't actually much left of her schedule tonight. That was the benefit of being chronically well organised, she supposed. When everything was planned and prepared in advance, she could just sit back and watch all the results of her hard work fall into place. Like with Will and Maya: the consequences of her plan had far exceeded her expectations, and she'd only had to intervene a couple of times to keep everything moving in the right direction. Better still, her boss had barely even noticed her involvement. The sign of a great executive assistant, she told herself. Her work was practically invisible.

She was so engrossed with watching the results of her meticulous planning she almost, *almost*, forgot where she was and what she was doing.

That was until a warm, rough fingertip found its way under her chin and tilted her face upward.

'Should I be worried about the competition?' Her eyes snapped back to his, and she was taken aback again by their intense colour, and the way he looked at her, as if there was some part of her he was trying desperately to see.

'So who were you watching?' he asked, reminding her of his question.

'Jealous?' She drew out the word with a smile, enjoying for a moment the control that it gave her. She didn't even know yet what she wanted to do with this blatant expression of interest, other than enjoy it for a moment. 'I'm just enjoying a plan coming together.'

'You planned that?' he asked, as her boss leant down and kissed Maya gently on the lips. The kiss itself was chaste enough, but the blatant bedroom eyes on both sides nudged it towards obscene.

'I may have helped a little.'

'Well, I prefer your attention here,' he said, attempting to soften his words with a cheeky grin.

'Demanding, much?' Okay, so her attention wasn't such a ridiculous thing to expect. But she didn't want him thinking he could just demand what he wanted and expect her to deliver. And she still wasn't sure how she felt about his attention. Attracted, sure. But meeting a party crasher with a cute smile and a devastating way of watching her hadn't featured in her plans for tonight. She'd had no advance warning, no time to think about what she wanted to do.

'Absolutely.' He remained completely straight-faced and Rachel recognised the challenge. 'But I think if you're going to agree to dance with me, it's only fair you give it your full attention.'

'Perhaps. But you're not holding up your end of the bargain. The dance was in exchange for an explanation. So spill. How did you get in without me knowing about it?'

'Grappling hook,' he replied, deadpan and with no hesitation. She let out a laugh, leaning back against his arm, letting the humour arch her body and soften her indignation.

He teased and she laughed, until she could feel the tension of the night leaching from her body. She'd not checked her watch since he'd led her to the floor, and she had no idea how long they'd been up there. And she was dangerously close to not caring. His humour, the naughty light in his eyes, was forcing the strain of preparing this evening from her limbs, demanding she enjoy herself. That she enjoy *him*. Eventually, when she'd laughed off his latest suggestion for how he'd joined the party—something about an international jewel thief—he leaned in close, until she could feel his warm breath disturbing her hair, and the minutest brush of his lips against her ear. With a little shiver, she suspected the time for games was coming to an end. 'Someone asked me to attend on their behalf. I couldn't say no. Are you going to throw me out?'

His reply prompted a hundred questions in her mind, but the one that sprang unguarded to her lips surprised even her: 'Where would you go if I did?'

His lips parted slightly and he chose his words carefully, she guessed, not wanting to break the connection crackling like electricity between them. 'That depends.'

Of course she was meant to ask 'on what', but the blatant suggestion in his eyes made her falter, suddenly aware they weren't playing any longer.

'Would you come with me?' he asked, deadly serious. He had given up on the dancing, too, and his hand had drifted up to her cheek, his thumb skittering across her skin. She had pulled her gaze away, unable to bear the close scrutiny of those huge, clear blue eyes, but now it snapped back up as she took a little half step away from him.

'I can't. I'm working.' She didn't even think before she spoke. The words came to her lips automatically as her heart rate spiked and her breath hitched. Her arms tensed where they rested against his body as she started to register the risk she'd taken coming up here with him. This man was chaos. She could see it in the haphazard drape of his tie and his mismatched cufflinks. The fact that even without being invited to the party he had got her away from her to-do list and onto the dance floor.

Her whereabouts and every action had been meticulously planned for the whole evening.

She'd been in the right place and at the right time, with the right files and figures for just about every one of the past eighteen hours. She was currently partway through the hour that she'd marked 'Networking, socialising, misc.' And when it came to an end, she had planned to run through a couple of details with the venue manager before leaving for the night. Alone.

Leo smiled at her, cool and relaxed.

'So you want to,' he said, as if he'd just gained a small victory.

She narrowed her eyes. She hadn't said that.

'You said you can't leave because you're working. But you never said you don't want to. I've been watching you all night. Waiting for the right moment to catch your attention; wanting to know what's on that tablet of yours. How you keep a party like this moving with just a whisper and a look in the right direction. I've been completely hypnotised by you and all I want for the rest of the night is to find out more.'

Her eyes widened in surprise; she was completely taken aback by his words.

She'd spotted him early in the night, and wondered which name his face belonged to. As she'd worked round the room, meeting and greeting, discussing the practicalities of donations, nudging Will in the right direction, and keeping the company CEO, Sir Cuthbert Appleby, happy, her thoughts had drifted to the guy in the slightly crumpled suit, his wavy hair resisting any attempt at a style. But the more her gaze had been drawn to him, the more she'd fought it, forcing her eyes to her work, her schedule and smartphone. She'd recognised the danger in that pull, the need to stick to her plan and see out the night as she'd intended. But now? This dance was perfectly in line with her itinerary. She'd always expected to do *some* socialising. And after that? She had ten minutes' work to do—tops.

So she could tell him she wasn't interested, that she had barely noticed him and didn't need to know any more than that. But it would be a lie. Because ever since his arm had captured her waist she'd been trying *not* to think about all the wicked things she'd like to do with his body. Her brain had thrown a dozen different suggestions at her, each one making her blush more than the last. Top of the list being to get his shirt off, so she could see if the contours of his body looked as good as they felt.

But she couldn't just take off with him. She had responsibilities here, she thought, her heart rate picking up again, though from desire or panic she couldn't tell. She had work she had to finish up. She couldn't just take off because—

Ooh.

His thumb continued its exploration of her jaw, and dipped into her collarbone in a way that made her melt.

When she looked up and met his eyes, the danger there was obvious. But he spelled it out for her, anyway.

'I want to make you shiver like that again,' he said slowly. 'I could try here, but...' He stroked that magic spot again and she bit the inside of her cheek to stop herself groaning out load.

'You see the problem?'

She nodded, but... 'I can't do this.'

'You can't? Or you don't want to?'

Did it matter? 'I have a plan for tonight.' She took another half step away from him, knowing she needed distance. 'This isn't it.'

He pulled her back in and rested his forehead against hers. 'Rachel, you're killing me. At least come somewhere we can talk.' His arm dropped from her waist abruptly, but before she could mourn its loss her hand was engulfed by his and she was striding with him across the ballroom.

When they reached the lobby, he whirled around, his lips stopping just inches from hers.

Was he doing it on purpose? Tempting her until she lost her mind and gave in?

'Help me here,' he said, his voice soft and enticing. 'You're attracted to me.' The lilt of his voice was just charming enough to compensate for his lack of modesty. 'So what's stopping you?'

She took her hand back, and a step away from him, understanding that being so close was doing nothing for her decision-making skills. This wasn't a question of what she wanted; she couldn't just drop everything and leave on a whim.

'Nothing's stopping me,' she said, keeping her voice carefully even. There was no need for him to know the nagging dread that would start in the base of her brain if she decided to embrace spontaneity. No need for him to know that she'd not done anything without a plan, a back-up plan and a contingency plan since she was a teenager. 'I'm working. I had some free time scheduled, and thank you for the dance, but now I have to get back.'

He looked at her carefully, and she held his gaze. 'Do you always have a plan? A schedule?'

'I do. What's wrong with that?'

'Oh, you mean except for the claustrophobia, the inflexibility, the stifling—' Wisely, he stopped himself, probably remembering he should play to his audience. 'So I wasn't in your plan for tonight. But what if something unexpected comes up? That must happen sometimes, right? Meetings get cancelled, things run late. Contracts get lost in the post. What happens to your plans then?'

'I make a new one,' she said, wondering what was behind his cut-off outburst, the flash of panic she'd seen on his face.

'You adapt to the circumstances—just like that. No stress. No panic.'

'Of course.' Working with Will could—and frequently did—send crises her way. She smoothed each problem until it fitted neatly into her existing plans, and all without anyone seeing that below the surface she was paddling like a racing swan.

Leo smiled at her as if he'd just scored a point. 'So make a new plan for tonight. Nothing serious, no reason to change tomorrow's plans, or any day after that. Just reschedule a couple of hours tonight to fit me in.'

'A couple of hours?' She raised an eyebrow at that: one night suited her just fine—her life was too full for anything more—but she had ideas enough already to fill more than a couple of hours. If she was going to do this, she was going to be sure it was worth her while.

And she was intrigued, because he was right. She'd altered plans before. She'd adapted to circumstances. Allowed for last-minute changes. So why shouldn't she do that tonight? Through the window into the ballroom she caught sight of Will and Maya dancing and remembered what she'd felt earlier, that stab of curiosity, or loneliness, or… Perhaps the fact that she didn't even know what it was made a good enough reason to do this.

'I have a few things I have to finish up before I—'

With a smile, he swooped in and pressed a quick, hard kiss to her lips. 'Just tell me when.'

CHAPTER TWO

LEO CRACKED AN eyelid and spotted a tangle of brown hair on the pillow beside him. Relaxing his head back, he was assailed by a stream of memories from the night before. Rachel meeting him outside the ballroom, belting her coat, telling him a cab was waiting for them. Him pressing a kiss to her neck as she unlocked her front door, too impatient to wait until they were inside. Her peeling off the silk of her dress with a teasing glint in her eyes.

He should be getting going, he thought, knowing that waiting round till breakfast could build unreasonable expectations that he might stay till lunch, and then dinner and then… His shoulders tensed, reminding him why breakfast was always a bad idea. Before he knew it, he could find himself trapped by expectations, unable to see his way out. The weight of claustrophobia sat on his chest as he remembered that feeling, of being stuck in a situation he couldn't escape. Locked in a dorm with people who only wanted to cause him hurt. But that wouldn't happen with Rachel, he reminded himself. She didn't want to lock him into anything. They were both happy with just one night. It had been hard enough to persuade her to find a few hours.

A snuffling noise came from beneath the mass of hair, and he smiled, despite himself. Running out of the door might be the safest option—and he wanted that Exit sign well in sight—but as he was hit by more flashbacks, he realised staying could definitely have its advantages.

He glanced around the bedroom, half lit by the summer sun fighting the curtains, and noticed for the first time the neatly arranged furniture, coasters on the bedside tables, books on the shelf organised by size, not a hairbrush or handbag or discarded running shoe in sight. The only items out of place were the trail of clothes from door to bed. So she'd not been faking the control-freakery. He felt a twist of unease again in his belly at what that might mean, whether that control would be heading his way. But he'd been pretty clear last night that he was only after a bit of fun—and she'd been equally frank about not being able to clear more than one night from her schedule for him.

Then a smooth calf rubbed against his leg, and any thoughts of running for the door vanished. Rachel turned her head on the pillow, and he watched her face as her eyes blinked, waiting for the moment when they finally opened properly and focused on him.

'Hi.' The sensation of her skin on his was making him impatient, and he wondered if it normally took her this long to come round.

'Morning.' She spoke the word quickly, shaking her head and blinking, as if rapidly assessing the situation and devising several different scenario-dependent plans. And she pulled the duvet up higher, tucking it tight against her breasts. A bit late for that, Leo thought. There was nothing he hadn't seen last night. More memories washed over him. Her skin, her taste, her smell.

'Forget I was here?' he asked, with a grin, propping himself up on one elbow.

'I thought maybe…' She flipped over and rubbed at her eyes, still sending him cautious looks, in between glancing at the door. Which told him exactly what she was thinking—the same as he'd been thinking not long before. 'Never mind.' She smiled, a little shyly, and glanced at the window. 'I need to be getting up.' She sat up properly and reached for her phone beside the bed, checking the time. At least he hoped that was all she was checking. He wasn't sure he could take it if she was kicking him out so she could deal with email.

'It's the weekend—what's the rush?' He wrapped his arm around her waist under the cover and pulled her back to him, grinning as she relaxed slightly. He took advantage of her momentary acquiescence and leaned over her, pinning her in place with an arm either side of her.

'I think you should stay,' he murmured soothingly, suddenly feeling as if nothing was as important as convincing her to spend a few more hours with him. It must be the sex, he told himself—the promise of a repeat performance—that had him so desperate to stay. Nothing to do with the cold and hurt he'd felt when she'd pushed him away—emotionally, if not physically—just now. He leaned in closer, brushed his lips softly against hers. When he thought he had her attention, he tucked a lock of her hair behind her ear.

'We could pretend it's not morning yet.' He glanced at the window, where the sun was still making a concerted effort to reach them. She held his gaze for a long moment, and he could see that light in her eyes that told him she was coming up with a plan. He grinned, suddenly excited to know what she would come up with.

'Well, maybe I could do with a little more sleep,' she said with an exaggerated yawn.

He laughed. 'Minx. Shut your eyes, then. Pretend it's still night.' Instead of closing them, she gave him a shrewd glance. Evaluation, he guessed. Assessing what this loss of control would cost her, and what she might stand to gain. Amending those plans of hers. He trailed a hand up the silky skin of her thigh, reminding her.

The moan that escaped her lips soothed his ego and brought a smile to his face.

Her eyelids drifted softly shut.

'Still feeling sleepy?'

'Maybe not quite sleepy…'

Afterwards, he held on to her tight. It was only as his eyes were drifting shut again that he remembered he'd planned to leave after…well, after.

'Ahem.'

At the clearing of her throat he forced his eyes open, drank in the colours of her hair, mahogany, chestnut, teak, which pooled in the hollow above her collarbone.

'Don't you need to…er…?'

He raised an eyebrow. Was she trying to kick

him out? Again? He tried to pull her closer, made an indiscriminate soothing noise, but she wriggled from his grasp.

'I'm getting up. If you want the bathroom first…'

'Right.' No cuddling, no morning-after awkwardness or expectations. This was what he wanted, he reminded himself, fighting a sense of disappointment.

She watched his back, well, more specifically, she ogled his bottom, as he walked to the bathroom. Then dropped her head back on the pillow and draped her arm across her face, blocking out the world. Okay, so she'd made some slight adjustments to her plans last night—and this morning. But there was no reason not to get back on schedule now.

And she and Leo knew where they stood—they'd both been very clear last night exactly what was on the table. Now it was morning, properly morning, they could go their separate ways and enjoy the memories. Apart. Safe. With no plans to meet again. Because adapting to change once was just plenty, thank you, however nice the results might have been; but the thought of approaching more than one night with Leo, and the chaos and disorder she was sure followed him everywhere, started a cool mass of dread deep in her belly. It had been years, longer than she could remember, since she had approached life without an itinerary—and even contemplating what that might feel like now made sweat prickle on her forehead.

Hearing the flush of the toilet and not wanting to be in bed when Leo came out of the bathroom, she grabbed clothes from the dresser, hiding herself away in soft black yoga pants and a draped sweater.

By the time the shower stopped she'd picked up and folded their clothes, straightened the nightstand on his side of the bed, and stripped the sheets. She was just about to grab a fresh set when the bathroom door opened and Leo appeared, wet from the shower, his face grim.

'We might have a bit of a problem.'

'What sort of a problem?' Though she could guess from his serious look that she wasn't going to like what he had to say.

'The condom—it broke.'

'Broke?' She tried to keep her voice below a screech, but wasn't sure that she managed it. 'What do you mean it broke?'

'I mean the condom had a tear in it. I thought you would want to know.'

She dropped the pillow she was holding and sat down heavily on the bed. Rubbing her fists against her eye sockets, she tried to take the information in and formulate a plan for what to do next. When she finally looked up, Leo was still standing in the doorway, watching her, a concerned look on his face.

'Are you on the pill?'

'No,' she said firmly, picking up her phone and jabbing at the screen. 'I'm not. But I'll stop at a pharmacy on my way to work and get the morning-after pill.'

She then nudged him gently out of the bathroom doorway with her hip.

'The door's just on the latch,' she said, desperate to be alone to gather her thoughts, and sure that Leo must be wanting to leave by now. She hadn't expected him to stay even this long. 'You can just pull it closed on your way out. Last night was lovely.' She turned and reached up to kiss him gently on the cheek then shut the door behind her.

She went about her Sunday-morning routine with meticulous precision, determined to banish the butterflies left over from her going off-plan last night with the familiarity of her routine. Shower, exfoliate, hair mask, face mask, cuticle oil. The appearance of a slightly scruffy-looking man with the ability to keep her awake half the night didn't mean her pores or her nails had to suffer.

It served as a timely reminder that she probably should have stuck to her plan A last night. Having a plan B was all good and well, but that didn't mean one always had to use it. Responding to change was part of her job, but a plan was meant to create order, not the chaos that threatened at the edges of her morning.

She emerged from the bathroom half an hour later with face, body and mind scrubbed smooth. And nearly dropped her towel at the sight of Leo stretched out on her unmade bed, eyes shut, breathing heavily, with two cups of coffee and a plate of toast on a tray beside him. Looking outrageously tempting. If it wasn't for the unease that gripped her shoulders, she might have been tempted to join him for round three. Instead she closed the door loudly, trying to wake him. He didn't stir. Clutching her towel more tightly, she walked over to the bed and reached out to shake him. But his fingers captured her wrist before she could touch him.

'What are you doing here?' she asked, too genuinely surprised to try and sugar-coat her words.

'You asked me back here. You had a plan, remember?' She smiled, trying to convince her shoulders there was no reason for them to tense and bunch up.

'No, I mean, why are you *still* here?'

'How about because I'm enjoying your company?' He reached and stretched behind him, then propped himself on his elbow, watching her from the bed as if he had every right to be there.

'I've not been keeping you company. I've been in the bathroom.'

'For an *age*. I know. What were you doing in there?'

'Grooming,' she replied with a quick, accidental glance at his tangle of hair, the stubble on his chin, the wrinkled shirt.

'Meow.' He laughed as he sat up on the unmade bed and reached for a coffee. 'Are you always this mean in the morning?'

'Are you always this annoying?'

Her scowl cracked into a grin as she sat beside him.

'This will help.' She reached for the other cup of coffee and took a long gulp. 'And then I really do have to go. I have things to do at the office.'

'The office? You know it's a Sunday, right? I saw your boss last night. I bet he's not going to be racing out of bed to get to work.'

'Quite. All the more reason why I have to. I had to put a few things on the back burner in the lead-up to the fundraiser. I want to get them moving again.'

'They'll still be there tomorrow. I, on the other hand…'

'Will be long gone—you were quite adamant about that last night, I remember. And yet here you are, holding me up when I want to get to work.'

'You work too hard.' The deliberate change of subject wasn't lost on her.

'Do you work at all?' she asked, genuinely curious, and realising now how little she knew about him. Other than that he likely had a rich benefactor, of course.

He nodded as he took a gulp of coffee. 'Sort of.'

'Sort of? Anyone I know who "sort of" has a job has mainly been occupied spending a trust fund.'

He winced, she noticed.

'So when you say "sort of", you don't have an actual job.'

'You could say that.' His grin told her that he was enjoying frustrating her, refusing to spill the details of his life. Not that it mattered to her what he did or didn't do, she reminded herself. It was just she was curious, having spent the night with a man to whom the very idea of a plan near on brought him out in hives.

'So how do you fill your days? When you're not attending gala dinners, that is.'

He gave her a carefully nonchalant look. 'I spend it at the beach.'

She nearly snorted her coffee with a good-natured laugh. 'Well, I should have guessed that,' she said, draining the dregs.

She hunted in her drawers for underwear and grabbed a simple shift dress from the wardrobe and then headed into the bathroom. When she emerged, dressed and perfectly coiffured, Leo was leaning against the kitchen counter, jacket and shoes on, the smile gone from his eyes.

'I didn't want to just disappear. I could walk you to the train? I have to get going.' He hoped his voice sounded less conflicted than he felt. That he wasn't giving away his battle between regret and impatience. Leo Fairfax didn't do regrets. He was walking away because it was the only way to be safe. The only way to ensure he didn't find himself in a situation that was intolerable, as he had at school. As much as last night and this morning had been exhilarating, wonderful, this had to end now.

He'd been perfectly frank last night that she shouldn't expect anything lasting from him.

'A walk to the station would be good. Are you ready to go?'

Leo reached for her hand as they walked along the leafy street, and wound his fingers with hers. It was only when he felt her hesitation, the tension in her muscles, that he realised what he'd done. He didn't do holding hands. He didn't do *Shall I walk you to the station?* because that led to expectation, and that was the very last thing that he wanted.

One morning like this led to another and another, until it became impossible to escape. But her hand felt right in his, her delicate, smooth palm lost in his huge, calloused, weather-worn grip. This was a choice, a pleasure, and he couldn't make himself take it back or regret it. He let go briefly as they passed through the ticket barrier, and had to stop himself from wrapping an arm around her waist as they walked through the station.

'I go north here,' she said eventually, when they reached the stairs. 'You want the southbound train, right?'

'Right.' He hesitated, no more willing to walk away from her now than he had been earlier in the morning. He tightened his hand around hers for a moment, the thought of waving her off causing an unexpected and unfamiliar pang. How could he want to keep hold of her and yet fear being tied to her at the same time?

Rachel wouldn't settle for someone drifting in and out of her life on a whim or desire. Whoever she decided to share her life with, she'd want him as predictable as the tide—she'd never stake her luck on waves and weather.

If he wanted more of her, it would mean dates and calendars and plans. And contingency plans and comparing schedules and an itinerary agreed months in advance. The thought of those constrictions, of being tied into someone else's expectations, demands... suddenly it was hard to breathe.

Since the day he'd left school, he hadn't encountered anything, whether it was a woman, a job, or the thought of family, that had made him want to tie himself down, to trap himself into any situation where he didn't have a clear and easy way out. He'd spent too many years in a hell he couldn't escape, trapped in a boarding house with his bullies, and no one to listen to him, to believe him. And all the time, the person he should have been able to go to for help, the person who should have been unquestionably on his side, had been the ringleader.

He'd counted down the days until he could leave school on his calendar, and then had never used one again. He'd sworn that he would never allow himself to be trapped as he was at school. Never find himself in a situation where someone had the power to hurt him, and he couldn't get away. So why was he gripping Rachel's hand as if she were a life buoy to a drowning man?

When he looked over at her fidgeting on her heels, all the reasons he knew he should walk away seemed to fade. He knew the dangers, knew that he couldn't hold on and expect to live untethered. He couldn't *want* a future with her in it, but his body refused to accept it. He turned to her, until they were shoulder to shoulder and toe to toe, just millimetres separating their bodies. He could feel the draw of her skin, pulling him towards her, and his fingertips brushed against her cheekbones of their own accord. As his hands moved to cup her face, to turn her lips up to meet his, a screech of brakes broke into his thoughts. He glanced across and saw the train pull up to the southbound platform.

'I have to go.' The words came from his lips, though he couldn't make himself believe them. But the train doors were closing, and with every piercing electronic beep he felt the walls of the station draw closer, his escape window closing.

With a wrench that he felt deep in his gut, he swept his lips across hers, pulled his hands away and then jogged down the stairs and through the doors of the train before either of them had a chance to say another word.

Rachel stood at the top of the stairs, watching as the train, and Leo, left the station. It was what she had wanted—him gone, and everything back to normal. But watching his train pull out of the station, she recognised the panicky feeling in her chest. He was gone, and she had no way of getting in touch with him. Despite everything, all the reasons she'd given herself that letting him into her life was a bad idea, despite the sense of panic that the thought of that man in her life caused, she wanted more of it. More of him.

Something caught her attention from the corner of her eye, and she started when she realised her train had already pulled up to the platform. She raced down the stairs, but the doors shut and locked with her on the wrong side. Even on his way out of her life Leo was disrupting her schedule. On second thought, she mused, maybe it was a good thing she wasn't in touch with him. He'd caused quite enough chaos in the one night she'd known him. She glanced up at the information screen, wondering how long the next train would be. Typical Sunday service. She'd be stuck on the platform for an hour.

But maybe she could do something useful with the time. A quick search on her phone showed a pharmacy just around the corner that should be open. Walking quickly, she headed to the chemist—a few minutes and several rather personal questions later, she had emergency contraception and a bottle of water. She read quickly through the information on the packet as she waited in a quiet corner of the station. Ninety-five per cent effective. Not ideal—but in the circumstances, the best she was going to get. She swallowed the pill then forced the issue from her mind, and looked through both hers and Will's schedules for the next week.

There were a couple of things she'd need to look into once she got to the office. Meetings that had been added at the last minute, when she was too busy with organising the fund-raiser to pull together all the research and paperwork that she knew Will would need in order to prepare.

She worked through a few of her emails, making adjustments to her plan for the week as she went and slotting in new items for her Monday morning meeting with Will.

After the meeting she'd be able to plan out the rest of her week almost to the last minute. And her regular 'contingency' and 'AOB' slots meant that even the unexpected would have to bend to her plans and not the other way around.

She'd come to rely on that order, needed those careful plans to make her feel safe. Because without them what else was there?

It had been the only way for years that she'd been able to quiet her feelings of chaos and panic. The men who'd broken into her childhood home hadn't planned to hurt anyone, the court had heard: they'd thought the house would be empty, had no idea that a fourteen-year-old Rachel was home alone. So when she'd startled one of them as he'd been rifling through the video collection, he'd panicked and lashed out at her. It was a pretty unpleasant knock to her head, but nothing serious. And eventually the nightmares she'd suffered had stopped, but that hadn't stopped her parents' guilt at leaving her at home. They'd fussed and smothered and, on occasion, wailed, insisting that Rachel inform them of her whereabouts at all times. Curfews were to be observed to the minute, unless she wanted to afflict a full-on panic-attack melt-down on her parents.

So she could be flexible if she had to be. 'AOB' and 'unexpected' had their own places in her plans, and that was all last night had been. But perhaps she shouldn't do it again. Those slots should be kept strictly for emergencies. Not for blonds who were hard to forget in the morning.

CHAPTER THREE

RACHEL SCROLLED THROUGH the next two weeks of Will's schedule, looking for a half-hour slot. She knew that she'd pencilled it in somewhere, knowing that this phone call would come at some point. Ah, there it was. The seventeenth. How could she have forgotten that? She put the details into the calendar, added links to the relevant paperwork on the servers, made sure that everyone involved in the project was copied into the invitation and saved everything. She smiled to herself, satisfied with her work. She'd been an executive assistant at Appleby and Associates, a financial services company in the city, for more than five years and prided herself on always knowing what Will needed before he did. If only everything was that easy, she thought, glancing again at the date. It won't change, she told herself. It doesn't matter how many times you look at it. She sat still and shut her eyes for a moment, concentrating on her body, not sure what she hoped, or even wanted to feel. Anything other than the hint of queasiness in her stomach and tiredness in her bones that had started to feel permanent. For the past week, seven full days since her period should have arrived, every day had been a whole load of nothing. And this after a half-hearted, barely-there appearance last month.

How long did she wait? she wondered. A week wasn't that big a deal, was it? She'd been busier than ever since that night—with Will's eye somewhat off the ball now he actually had a personal life. And then he and Maya had started coming up with more and more fundraising ideas to support the charity, and it felt as if she hadn't had a moment to herself since then. It was just the stress. Except she wasn't stressed. She'd just worked the new projects into their routine and it had been fine. She wasn't stressed; she was just late. And it seemed like a little too much of a coincidence that the first time she'd ever been late coincided with her first ever sexual wardrobe malfunction. That ninety-five-per-cent figure had been haunting her thoughts for six days now.

She should probably talk to Leo, she thought. But she hadn't asked for his number that night—could she face calling his father, whose gala invitation he had taken, to try and get hold of him?

At least at the moment she had nothing to tell. But she couldn't leave it that way for long. She needed to know what she was dealing with. If—and it was still a big one—but if she was pregnant, then the sooner she knew, the sooner she could formulate a plan. It was twelve-thirty now, which gave her enough time to nip to the chemist's around the corner, grab a pregnancy test and a sandwich, and be back at her desk well before Will's two o'clock meeting. She locked her computer and grabbed her bag from her drawer, then headed out of the building.

Twenty minutes later she locked the cubicle door and sat on the lid of the toilet, reading through the packet instructions.

Pee, wait, read. And then she'd know.

She peed. She waited. The seconds on her phone stopwatch ticked by slowly, as if the whole universe wanted to put this off as much as she did.

At twelve fifty-nine she took a deep breath, closed her eyes for that last, long second, and then looked at the stick.

Pregnant.

She could barely see as she walked—dazed—out of the bathroom. She stopped at the coffee machine, as was her habit after lunch, and as she was about to select her usual order she stopped herself, blinked a couple of times, and selected decaf instead. She reached for the cup and took a sip, and felt the relief and comfort of her routine in place of the caffeine rush.

'Got the jitters?'

She whipped around at the sound of that familiar voice and felt the blood drain from her face.

'Leo, what a—'

She couldn't finish the word, never mind the sentence. What was he doing here? Why today? Why right now? Why did he have to look even better than she remembered? Sun-bleached, tanned and twinkling with humour.

He was watching her with careful eyes. And he reached out and took the cup from her shaking hands. 'Are you okay?' he asked. 'I didn't mean to startle you. But you looked as if you were in a world of your own.'

'No, it's… It's… Leo?'

He gave her a smug grin, and that helped her regain her senses somewhat. He wouldn't be looking at me like that if he knew what I knew, she thought. If he knew that in a few short months he'd be dad to a bouncing baby boy or…

She felt her blood drain lower still, and had to lean back against the counter in the small kitchen to keep her balance. Leo took a step closer and set the coffee down beside her, before taking her hand and looking closely at her face.

'You're white as a sheet,' he said. 'I'd love to take the credit for you swooning and all, but I'm worried. Are you ill? Should I call someone?'

'No, no,' she said, trying to regain composure amid the rush of her thoughts and the swirl of sensation from his fingertips. 'I'm surprised, that's all. And in need of a coffee.'

'So why are you drinking decaf?'

Great, she thought. Walked straight into that one. 'Because I've already drunk too much today, and know that I'll need a proper one before this afternoon's over.' Hopefully that would allay any more questions. She moved forwards tentatively, moving her weight from the counter to her feet, and almost smiled before she felt herself sway slightly. She really should have eaten that sandwich before taking the test, she thought. Because right now, despite her achingly empty stomach, and rather light head, she was sure she wouldn't be able to keep even a mouthful down.

'That's it, you're not well,' Leo declared, eyeing her carefully. 'You need to take the afternoon off.' She gave a shaky laugh, tensing slightly at this reminder of Leo's cavalier attitude to a nine-to-five.

'I'm fine, honestly. I've just not had lunch yet.'

'Then let me walk you to your desk, at least.'

'Leo, please, just leave it.'

This wasn't fair. She was careful. She was always careful. And then when events had conspired against her, she'd gone straight to the pharmacy and taken that pill. Why did *she* have to be that five per cent?

She had to tell him. He had a right to know. They had a right to make any decisions that needed to be made together. But did she have to do this just now, before she'd even had a chance to get used to it herself?

Leo was standing in front of her, close, too close, and she needed space to think about this. But she couldn't do that, because her calendar was full all afternoon. And all of tomorrow, and the day after that. Every minute of every day was accounted for. And she liked it like that; she just wished that she'd known to schedule in time to adjust to pregnancy, to becoming a mother. At that thought her knees went, and even though it was only for a second she knew that Leo had seen it. He slipped his arm around her.

'Where's your desk?' he asked.

She laid her hand on his at her waist, grateful for the support, but well aware that she couldn't be half carried through her office. She took a deep breath, let it out slowly, and grabbed hold of her self-control. She pushed Leo's arm away gently and stood up, forcing her heels into the floor, and walked across to her desk. Leo followed beside her looking concerned, but not trying to touch her.

'So what are you doing here?' she asked when she was safely back at her desk, looking for any excuse to draw the conversation away from herself. 'You probably should have called first—I try and keep my personal life away from work.'

He gave her an assessing look and then leant back against her desk.

'One, I couldn't have called because you didn't give me your number. And two, as delightful as it's been running into you, I'm not here to see you.'

'Oh.' Just when she'd thought this day couldn't get any worse. She thanked her forethought in ordering a perfectly fitted ergonomic chair that wouldn't allow her to slump with disappointment even if she'd wanted to. Which, she told herself strictly, she absolutely didn't.

'Seeing you is just a very pleasant bonus,' he

added with a hot smile that softened her disappointment, reminded her of that night and reached right to her belly. 'And as you haven't eaten, can I take you for lunch?'

'I've…I've already taken my lunch break. And if you're not here to see me, then surely you have plans.'

'Right,' he said slowly, as if only just remembering. 'I have a meeting with Will.'

'No, you don't.'

He laughed out loud. 'I promise you I do. I called him this morning, told him I was in town unexpectedly. He wanted a chat about something I mentioned at the fundraiser so we said we'd grab a few minutes this afternoon. I'm sorry, should I have checked with you first?'

'No, of course not. Will, however—'

'Is the boss—last time I checked.'

She spun round at the sound of Will's voice.

'And entirely dependent on my secretarial talents. And knows how much I *love* surprises.'

'Well, that's me told.' Will laughed, reaching out to shake Leo's hand. 'Sorry I'm a few minutes late, and, as I'm sure Rachel has already told you, I have another meeting in twenty minutes. But we can talk through a couple of ideas if you like and then follow up over Skype?'

'Perfect,' Leo said. 'And then Rachel and I are going to head out for a bite to eat. Assuming that's not a problem with the boss.' Her eyes whipped to him, and her jaw dropped open at the sheer cheek of it.

'No problem at all,' Will said, with a raised eyebrow in her direction. 'I assume everything's set for my two o'clock?'

Professional pride forced her not to snap at either one of them. 'Files are on your desk, electronic copies are attached to the calendar appointment. The access codes for the tele-conferencing are in there, too, but I can dial in for you if you need me to.' She fought the urge to tell Leo to sod off. Because much as his heavy-handed interference with Will ran-kled, if she didn't go now, then when was she going to tell him? It needed doing, and she'd be surprised if she was presented with a bet-ter opportunity than this.

'No, it's fine. I'm sure I can manage on my own for a couple of hours, despite what you might think. You go, enjoy yourself,' he said with a smirk that told her she was definitely not forgiven for interfering with his love-life.

Rachel looked pointedly at the clock. 'Your next meeting is in fifteen minutes, Will. Do I need to contact everyone and let them know it'll be late starting?'

He laughed, and she cursed the permanent good mood he'd been in since the night of the fundraiser. He had been so much easier to manage before. And she had no one to blame but herself.

'Come on through, Leo,' he said, with a smile in his voice that matched the grin on his face.

Rachel busied herself working through straining inboxes, her own, Will's, as well as one of the generic admin accounts. Then she flicked through her hard-copy inbox, separating out her own items from Will's, checking that the assistants had marked the correct pages for him to sign, adding sticky tabs where they hadn't. Finally she tackled the outbox, dividing up the signed documents into the recipients they needed to be sent to next. The second hand on the clock above Will's door crawled round, until she was certain that physics was working against her.

Except this was what she wanted, wasn't it? To put this off—for ever, if that were an option. She didn't want to see Leo. Didn't want to have lunch with him. She wanted to never see him again, never feel the loss of control that she'd experienced that night. And that had had consequences just as frightening as she'd ever imagined.

A baby. Where was she meant to fit a baby into her life? The Friday-afternoon 'catching up with the trade press' hour? She wasn't exactly experienced at motherhood, but she was pretty sure that a baby needed more than an hour a week. Even if she pulled together every single one of her contingency and emergency hours it was less than a day a week. No, having this baby meant ripping up everything that made her feel safe and secure, and starting over completely. She leant back in her chair, surveying the piles of paperwork covering her desk. What was the point to this? Because it wouldn't matter how neat the piles, how precise and efficient her system. At some point, this would all fall apart.

She had choices. She didn't have to do this, to have this baby. But even as she thought it, the tearing pain in her heart told her that it wasn't the right choice for her.

She was having this baby.

Now she just had to tell Leo.

She glanced up at the clock again—one-fifty-eight—and wondered if Will would remember his call. Should she buzz through and remind him? So that he didn't run late or so that she could get to lunch with Leo? She didn't want to think too hard about the answer to that.

At two minutes past two the door opened

and Leo walked out, a grin still on his face. But then what did he have to worry about? Who wouldn't be happy if they could spend all day at the beach or dipping into their trust fund? Well, he might have to think about getting a little responsibility after today.

If he wanted to be involved, that was. She should really have used this time to think about what she was going to tell him, what she was going to ask him. What she wanted from him. She didn't need him to do this. Frightening as it was, she knew it could be done alone. There were plenty of single mothers out there who balanced parenthood with careers. No doubt all that was needed were killer organisation skills, and she had that one wrapped up nicely.

She refused to look up at him, still annoyed with Leo for his heavy-handedness. Instead she kept her eyes firmly on her monitor as she continued with her work. But she hadn't counted on a blond head with tanned skin and insanely blue eyes intruding into her field of vision.

'Ready to go?' Leo asked as he leaned nonchalantly forward and against her cubicle.

'Su-u-u-re,' she replied, buying herself extra milliseconds by dragging out that one syllable for as long as she could without seeming ridiculous. She saved and closed her documents, backed everything up, flicked through her inbox to make sure that nothing urgent had arrived in the past five minutes, and then logged off. She took a sneaky deep breath as she reached under her desk for her handbag and braced herself. She was going to tell him. That was non-negotiable. What happened after that, how Leo reacted, she had zero control over.

Her stomach churned and she wished that she could blame it on morning sickness, but this was just good old-fashioned nerves.

'Will told me about this great place around the corner,' Leo said as they walked out of the door and onto the street. Great. He was definitely interfering and it was definitely on purpose.

How was she supposed to do this? Did she just blurt it right out over starters? Ply him with wine beforehand to soften the blow? Maybe she should tell him before they even sat down—that would make it less embarrassing if he did a runner straight off.

And she couldn't even have a glass of wine to steady her nerves.

Before she had a chance to realise how far they had walked they were passing through the doors of the restaurant and being shown to their table. Somehow in their fifteen-minute meeting, either he or Will had found a moment to call ahead. Perfect.

Now she sat trying to surreptitiously watch him over the top of her menu. He was in a good mood, and a smile was lighting up his face. She wondered at the reason for it. Was it the meeting with Will that had made him happy, or was it sitting here with her? She wasn't sure she wanted to know the answer. She didn't want to enjoy this, or for him to. Relationships meant chaos; they meant accommodating another person—something she generally didn't do outside a boss-employee relationship. And even then she only worked with people who were really looking for her to manage them, rather than the other way around. So she indulged in friendships and occasional casual dalliances, knowing that she could get out the minute anything approaching chaos started to impinge on her life. Short flings were satisfying and easy to manage. Leo fitted beautifully into that first category, but was failing miserably with the second.

He looked up and caught her eye.

'So, anything you fancy?' he asked with a cheeky grin. She rolled her eyes at the lazy innuendo. He slouched back in his chair and she took a moment to really look at him, in a way she hadn't allowed herself since the hazy early-morning hours after the fundraiser. She was desperate to smooth the chaotic curls that tumbled rebelliously over his forehead, but was aware at the same time he'd lose something of his charm if she were to do it.

Drawing her eyes away from him, she toyed with a breadstick as they waited in silence for the main courses to arrive. This was bad. This was a bad date. *She* was a bad date. How had she spent hours with this man, making love as if it were the most natural thing in the world, and now she was struggling to make small talk?

'Is everything okay?' Leo asked.

So her complete state of panic hadn't gone entirely unnoticed. Well, the worried glances he'd been throwing at her for the past fifteen minutes should have been her first clue. She'd chosen to studiously ignore them, worried that acknowledging them would lead to talking about what was wrong. But still, she was surprised by the serious note to his voice, feeling his concern, the connection between them, all the way to her core. She remembered the way she had felt that morning at the railway station, watching his train pull away from the platform and knowing that however much she felt for him, she'd missed any opportunity to explore it. And then he'd waltzed back into her life on the day when exploring any connection between them seemed more impossible than ever.

She had to tell him, and now was as good a time as any. Actually, no, that wasn't true. Now was the best chance she was going to get. She took a long, fortifying sip of her mineral water, wishing it could have been an ice-cold glass of Sauvignon Blanc, and opened her mouth to speak.

'Leo, there's something—'

'Here we go—two *tagliatelle al ragu*? Would you like parmesan? Black pepper?'

She hid her frustration behind a smile as the waiter bustled and chatted at them good-naturedly. And then watched his retreating back in panic, flailing.

'You were—'

'I'm pregnant.'

She blurted the words out before Leo could finish his sentence, and instantly regretted it as Leo snorted his red wine.

'Pregnant?'

'Keep your voice down,' she hissed, hoping that Will hadn't told anyone else at the office about this place.

'How can you be— I thought you were going to— What does— *Pregnant?*' She waited out his rambling until he could form a complete sentence. 'It's not even been that long,' he said.

'Only a few weeks. Can you even be sure? I mean, how do these things work?'

'It's been seven weeks. I'm late, I took a test, it was positive,' she said, trying to keep her temper, trying to remember that she'd not exactly been level-headed when she first found out, either. She couldn't be disappointed that he'd not taken it well—she'd not expected beaming smiles. But perhaps some tiny part of her had hoped for something…more. More than this obvious horror.

'Did you take the morning-after pill?'

'Does it matter? I'm pregnant.'

He leaned back in his chair and she tried to remind herself that actually, yes, it wasn't such an unreasonable question. After the condom fail, the contraceptive ball had been entirely in her court—there was nothing he could have done.

She softened her voice. 'Yes. I took it that morning, about half an hour after your train left. I followed the instructions and did everything right. But it's not a hundred per cent effective.' She gave him a minute to absorb this, but then found she didn't have anything else to say. She just waited for him to process.

'Are you okay?' he asked eventually, and she cracked a tiny smile, touched at the softness in his voice. She remembered it from that night.

'I'm still trying to take it in,' she said honestly.

'When did you find out?'

She checked her watch. 'A couple of hours ago. Right before—'

'Right before I surprised you at the coffee machine. Jeez, no wonder you were a mess.'

'A mess?'

'You know, all…' He waved a hand in the air, and she told herself it was probably better to be charitable and not to try and translate it.

'Have you thought about…?' From the careful way he spoke the words, and wouldn't look up to meet her eye, she knew what he was asking.

'I'm keeping it.'

As she said the words, she felt their truth. Felt that she could never give a different answer to that question. Parallel shivers of excitement and fear raced up her spine.

'You're keeping it,' he repeated, his intonation just hinting at a question. 'Isn't this something I should expect to have a say in?' he asked.

Rachel dropped her head into her hands and rubbed at her hair, unable to bear the intensity of his stare. 'I'm not sure it's the sort of thing you can compromise on. It's sort of an either-or situation.'

'Still,' Leo said, his expression bordering on haggard when she peeked up through her fingers. 'When did you decide this, if you only just found out? You can't have had time to think it through.'

'I haven't. I don't need to. I know some people would choose something different, and I totally respect the right to make that choice. But it's not what I want.' She couldn't explain the fiercely protective instinct that told her she had to keep this baby, but that didn't mean she didn't recognise it. It had been there, lurking, since the minute she'd read the word 'Pregnant' on the test. It was the reason she'd had decaf coffee, and the reason she'd told Leo now, without needing time to think through their options.

'Did you plan this?' Leo's question snapped her out of her thoughts in an instant, and cut straight to her heart. She gaped at him, affronted.

'Why in God's name would you think I *planned* this?' He sat back against his chair again, letting it take his weight as if he were no longer able.

'You plan everything else.' His expression was hard and guarded—she flinched from the anger and the hurt she could see simmering below the surface. She wouldn't stand for this.

This was not her fault. They had both played their part in getting them to this point, and they would both have to deal with the consequences. She opened her mouth to tell him that, but he spoke first. 'What was it—a big birthday on the horizon got your biological clock ticking? Did you reach the entry in your calendar that read "Start a family" and just pick up the next willing donor?'

She dropped her fork in shock, her mouth open as she tried—and failed—to put words to her hurt.

'Do you really think I'm capable of that?' Rachel asked, her voice low and throaty as she fought down tears, disbelieving that he could be capable of such cruelty. Of course she knew that she didn't know him *well*, but she'd thought after that night she had a pretty good measure of him. Nowhere had she seen the capacity for such heartlessness. 'Because I'm cutting you a hell of a lot of slack here by not throwing something.'

'No. I don't know. God.' He ran his fingers through his hair. 'I honestly don't know what to think. I turn up at your office hoping for a smile and a flirt and maybe—if I played my cards right—a repeat performance of that night. And you tell me that I'm going to be a father, whether it's what I want or not. I tell you, I've thought about you since that night, thought about you a lot, actually, but I never imagined…*this*.'

Rachel let out a long sigh. 'How could you? I can barely imagine it now, barely believe that it's true.' She took another long sip of her water and picked disconsolately at her congealing pasta. 'What are we going to do?'

She gave a little shudder at the sudden re-alisation she had no answer to that question. The next few months, years, decades of her life—which this morning had a predictable, reliable pattern—suddenly blurred, as she saw her plans for the future evaporating. To be re-placed with…what? She had no idea what the next few days looked like now, never mind anything beyond that. A fist of fear gripped her lungs, and she struggled to draw in a breath. When she finally managed to drag in a couple of gasps of oxygen, she found that they were stuck there. She tried to force them out, but the effort tightened her chest further. One hand flew to her shirt, pulling at the collar as if it would somehow help the air move.

Her movement must have startled Leo, be-cause his gaze flew from where it had been locked on the tablecloth to her face, and she saw her alarm reflected there. 'Rachel?' he asked urgently. 'What's wrong?' His hand reached for hers across the table.

'Can't…breathe…' she managed to gasp.

'Did you swallow something?'

She shook her head and saw realisation dawn in his eyes. He gripped her hand harder and pulled her from her seat, throwing some notes on the table and leading her quickly to the door. Once outside, he pulled her through the gates of a small park and down beside him onto a bench. He placed his hand firmly on her face, his palm cupping her cheek.

'Look at me,' he ordered her, his voice steady and understanding. 'Rachel?' Her darting gaze locked onto him.

'You can breathe just fine,' he told her, his eyes fixed on hers, his voice calm but firm. 'I'm going to count and you're going to breathe out. Then you're going to breathe in.' She nodded, willing herself to believe him, listening to his voice rather than the racing of her mind as he counted 'one…two…three…' With her lungs so full she thought they might burst, she looked at his eyes, focused on his words, the simplicity and predictability of the numbers, and let her chest relax, let go of the solid tightness of her shoulders and the terror in her mind. As she gradually felt her body return to normal, she slumped back on the bench, and Leo did the same.

'Thanks,' she managed eventually.

'Okay,' Leo said. 'I think one thing we have to agree on right now is that neither of us is particularly able to make important decisions at the moment.'

'I—'

'Just had a panic attack. Forgive me if I take that to mean we need a little time.' She nodded slowly, unable to dispute his words. This might be easier if she were doing it alone, she thought. If she could make a plan exactly as she wanted, and then stick to it.

She knew without question that life couldn't happen that way with Leo. He would throw her plans off course from the first possible moment, and insist on chaos as often as possible after that. Just the thought of it made her chest feel tight again.

'Do you have to go back to the office or can I see you home?' Not words to help her to breathe normally.

'I have to get back,' she said, thinking of her and Will's schedule for the afternoon. She couldn't just not turn up.

'We need to talk, properly,' Leo said, and reached for her hand—a spark of something half remembered flickered between their skin. Her first instinct was to snatch her hand back—his touch was too dangerous—but his fingers clamped around hers before she could. His other hand tucked her hair behind her ear, and smudged away a tear that was trickling over her cheek. He turned her to look at him, and she relaxed, thinking how easy it would be to lean forward, to brush her lips against his, to lose herself for a moment. Leo's breathing quickened, and she knew he'd thought it, too. But, she told herself, the last thing this situation needed was more complications.

She dropped her gaze and pulled back slightly.

'Perhaps we should talk in a few days, when we've had time to think…' Her voice tailed off as she tried to reshape her view of the world to imagine how that conversation would go. 'Are you coming up to London again?'

'No,' Leo said, with a small shake of his head. 'Not for a while. But you could come down to my place in Dorset, get away for a few days.'

Rachel opened her mouth to protest, but he held up a hand to stop her. 'Just hear me out. There's space, fresh air and distance from your office. I'm not promising sea air has all the answers, but maybe a change of perspective…?'

'I'm not sure that's a good idea.'

'And I'm not sure what choice we have. I can't see that getting to know each other is optional, now. I know where you live—where you work. I've even seen you in action. Don't you think it's fair that you see a little of my life, too?'

She nodded. 'Perhaps I could come for the day.'

'Honestly, by the time you've travelled, you'll want to stay longer,' Leo said. 'Plan to come at the weekend. Stay Saturday night. I have a guest room,' he added, no doubt noticing the refusal that was about to leave her lips.

She tried hard to think of some way to skewer this logic, some way to get out of this scenario that had her holed up with a man she found dangerously irresistible—the man who had got her pregnant. But whichever way she looked at it, she could see that he was right.

'Okay,' she said eventually. 'I'll come.'

CHAPTER FOUR

LEO COLLAPSED ONTO the sand, chest heaving and limbs comfortingly heavy.

A baby. He still couldn't quite connect that concept with his life. How had that even…? Okay, so it wasn't as if he needed a diagram, and it wasn't as if he didn't believe Rachel when she said she'd taken the morning-after pill. They were just that tiny fraction of a per cent that the maths for a double contraceptive fail worked out as. Maybe at the end of this weekend—he glanced at the sun; Rachel would be here in a few hours—it would feel more real.

He rubbed the heel of his hand against his forehead as he tried to think, the rhythmic crash of the waves on the sand soothing in its familiarity. Was *real*—knowing that there was absolutely, definitely no way of getting out of this—going to feel better? How could it? He'd all but walked away from his family. Had been happy managing on his own. But what could he do now? He'd enjoyed every minute of what had got them here, and he would take responsibility for what they'd done.

His head should be spinning. These past few days he should have wanted to scream, or run, or, God, *faint* or something. But instead, he felt nothing. A blank, empty space filled his brain, keeping feelings at bay.

But as he sat, thinking, he noticed a warm yellow glow creeping around the edges of that numb void. A hint of some emotion that was waiting, just out of reach, but heading closer.

He flopped back onto the sand, covering his eyes from the intense glare of the sun with his arm. Part of him wanted to go. To turn around and walk away and just imagine he'd never laid eyes on Rachel. Pretend that one night, one night that had tied him into a lifetime of commitment, had never happened. But then a flash of memory assailed him—a gentle, lazy smile on Rachel's lips in the dim early-morning light. Too tired for games, too sated for self-protection, he'd seen for the first time the real, unguarded woman, with no barriers, no motives, no second-guessing. He couldn't make himself regret that moment, that instant connection.

And there went the 'numb' phase, as the

memory of his desire and passion that night was chased from his body by nausea-inducing fear. He let out a long, unsteady breath. God, he wished he'd appreciated 'dazed' more.

For a moment the thought of that commitment, the inescapable permanency of it, threatened to paralyse him, bringing back every nightmare and the sleepless nights between. The last time Leo Fairfax had been this frightened of the future.

But he was going to be a father. He and Rachel—that fascinating, maddening, excessively disciplined woman he'd been unable to shake from his mind for *weeks* now, had somehow, against all her best-laid plans, and his lack of them, created a new human life. The magnitude of the realisation stole his breath for a few long moments as he looked up and out across the water, trying to imagine who he was, this whole new person that they had created. But the vision remained hazy, too unformed to be anything more than broad strokes of a life.

Rachel stepped out of the taxi—she'd insisted to Leo that she could, and would, get to his place under her own steam—and gasped in horror. He'd warned her on the phone that he was doing some renovations, but this was…it was ramshackle. The ground all around was either churned up or covered in bags of building materials, and the windows were still covered by plastic sheeting. Most concerning of all, the roof seemed to consist of a couple of blue tarpaulins, flapping gently in the breeze. She glanced up further, relieved to see that the sky was still a clear, sunny blue, without a cloud in sight.

Thank goodness she had a list of practically every hotel in Dorset, sorted by distance from the coastal village Leo's postcode had directed her to. And a list of taxi companies, too. And train times back to London. As she'd saved them all on her tablet, just in case she found herself out of network coverage, she'd hoped that she wouldn't actually need them. She wanted to use her time here to get to know Leo better—it was essential, in the circumstances. And staying in a hotel the whole weekend would mean less time together. But she wasn't sure that a building site was the best place to get to know each other, either.

She'd give it a chance, she told herself, but double-checked that she had signal on her mobile, just in case. Tentatively, she picked her way along the path from the road, and as it passed around the corner of the cottage she stopped and dropped her bag. Okay, so *this* she could stay for. The cottage was perched on top of a rocky cliff, with views all around the bay, from majestic, prehistoric coastline at one end to brightly coloured beach huts and umbrellas at the other. The clumpy grass she'd been cursing for catching on her heels gave way to sand and rocks, and a path meandered down to the narrow sandy beach.

She breathed in a couple of good lungfuls of sea air, but her brief moment of tranquillity was interrupted by a mechanical scream from inside the house. The noise made her jump, but—curious—she ventured towards the door, certain that a whole crew of builders must be in there to make such a racket. A troop of roofers, she hoped, casting another glance at the tarp.

'Hello?' she shouted, once she'd grappled with her bag and made it to the door.

But when she caught sight of Leo, she fell silent, leaning against the door frame to enjoy the view. He wore jeans—faded and worn, moulded to his body in a way that told her they were well loved and often worn. His T-shirt was white, damp down the back and clinging in all the right ways. The powerful swimmer's muscles of his shoulders and back were outlined by the soft cling of the jersey, and rippled as he handled planks of wood and an electric saw with ease.

All day her thoughts had flip-flopped between terror and excitement at the thought of seeing Leo again. They had drifted his way often in the weeks since she'd seen him, reliving that night over and over again. But it wasn't just the sex that had stuck in her mind. It was the way he'd smiled at her on the dance floor as he'd figured her out, and found which buttons to press to help her change her mind. The sparkle in his eyes as he'd watched her figure him out, and find a way to take him home.

It was the way she'd let go as she'd moved in his arms, following his lead, taking it back, following her body and his, improvising. Exploring every possibility thrown up by this totally unplanned—she could admit it to herself, if not to him—encounter. But the things she'd found with him that night were exactly the reason she was nervous now. How would she keep control over the rest of her life when she'd failed so spectacularly to keep control even over her own body?

Well, she told herself, the first defence was easy—no repeat performances. She had to keep her head. Which meant she had to put the brakes on this little ogling session and somehow get his attention. Not easy when he was wearing ear protectors and making an unholy racket.

It didn't seem wise to sneak up on a man when he was communing with the power-tool gods. But how long was she meant to stand there? How long could she watch him like this before her resolve began to falter? She was about to take a step forward when her gaze dropped from where it had been fixed on Leo, and her brain caught up with what her eyes were hinting was wrong with the picture. The floor—where was it? She hadn't noticed it immediately because Leo was standing on a large piece of board, but between the door and him—nothing. Well, not quite nothing. A few joists, the odd floorboard balanced across them. Otherwise, just bare earth a few inches down.

She snatched her foot back and switched to plan B. While she waited for him to finish what he was doing with the saw, she pulled her phone out of her pocket and found his number. As soon as the whine of the tool stopped, she hit Dial, hoping that he had his phone on him, and set to vibrate. It gave her the perfect excuse to look at his bottom at least—trying to see if it had started buzzing, of course.

As she watched, Leo straightened and stretched his muscles, and then reached into his back pocket. Was it her imagination, or did his shoulders tense when he lifted the phone and saw the display? Regardless, hers tensed, too—sympathy stress. When Leo wrenched off the ear protectors, she cleared her throat and he finally turned to look at her.

She tried to read his expression—in business, a degree of mind-reading came in handy. And while she hadn't quite cracked full-on ESP yet, she'd got pretty good at reading people. So she knew that the smile was genuine—but what he was feeling was more complex than his sunny grin implied. His mouth said he was happy to see her. The line of his shoulders and slight stiffness in his arms told her he was wary. Of her? Of the baby? Was there a difference any more? They came as a package deal—literally—for the next seven or so months.

But he was still smiling at her as he walked across the room—balancing on the joists like a gymnast on a beam.

'Hi,' he said as he got to the door. 'I wasn't expecting you yet. Sorry, I thought I'd be done for the day before you got here.' She glanced at her watch. According to her travel schedule, which she'd sent over to him yesterday, she was right on time. But perhaps it was a little early in the trip to bring that up. She remembered the way he had stiffened when he'd seen she was calling and almost flinched herself. It was hardly flattering, knowing she was the cause of such trepidation. And she had no desire to kick off with anything other than small talk just yet. She'd put in a lot of thought, time and energy over the past few days, trying to come up with a plan that would suit both of them, all three of them, for the foreseeable future. There were a few scenarios for them to choose from, but she was satisfied that between the notes on her tablet and the scenario-planning charts she'd printed and bound she'd come up with something that they could work with. All she had to do now was convince Leo of that fact, and in doing so she was going to have to tread lightly.

'Oh, it's fine,' she said, trying to be breezy about the lack of flooring. 'So…new boards?'

'It's kind of a work in progress,' Leo said, glancing about him, apparently unconcerned. 'We found some rot and had to rip the old ones out. Then I found these incredible boards at a rec yard.'

She smiled and nodded, feeling the tension in her shoulders travel down her arms until her fingers were fighting against tight fists.

'But isn't it a little…inconvenient—not having a floor?'

'It's only temporary.' He shrugged. 'And it's only one room—the rest of the house is fine. Are you coming in?'

Fine? From what she'd seen from the outside, this floor was the least of her worries. But she forced herself to take a deep breath, and keep her smile stuck on a little longer.

'Sure.' She grabbed the handle of her suitcase and looked at the floor in anticipation, mapping out the shortest and quickest route.

'Leave your case—I'll grab it. Isn't there a "no heavy lifting" clause in this pregnancy thing?'

Her eyes flicked to his face, trying to read his expression. It was the first time either of them had mentioned the baby, and his voice hadn't exactly sounded sure, almost as if he were testing the words, not quite believing them. She didn't answer. She couldn't, yet. Couldn't face up to all the uncertainties that lay ahead of them.

She set a foot on the joist by the door. A couple of steps in she started to wish she'd kicked off her shoes as she wobbled a little on her stiletto heel. But just as she started to worry that she might not get that wobble back under control, Leo's hand grabbed hers and held her steady. A shiver spread through her body at the feel of his hand, and she squeezed it tight, suddenly feeling less steady on her feet, not more. He swung the door open in front of them and she jumped across the last gap.

As she landed, she wobbled again, and this time Leo's arm caught her around the waist. She'd put out a hand to break the fall she'd been sure was inevitable, but instead of hitting the floor it hit solid, warm muscle. She should have snatched it back, of course. Should definitely not have stretched her fingers and pressed her palm a little tighter against him, remembering the night she had spent held against that chest, the salty taste as she'd kissed it, how she'd pressed her palms to it as she'd…

Leo's arm tightened around her and she wondered if he was remembering, too. She looked up and found his gaze intent on her, his eyes serious and the smile gone. Her lips parted, and her body begged her to stretch up, to press her lips against his, to lose herself in his body. But her brain screamed warnings thick and fast. Caught in the middle, she wavered, leaning back slightly against Leo's arm as she met his gaze. Over his shoulder, she caught a glance of the room they had just left—the chaos, the power tools, the almost complete lack of *floor*—and she took a deliberate step backwards. Her life was chaotic enough. One night with Leo had shaken up everything she thought she knew about the future and dumped it back around her. The last thing she needed at the moment was for that to happen again.

Leo gave her a long look, his expression neither regretful nor pleased, but hovering somewhere around wary. After a beat, he turned from her and strode back across the joists to rescue her case from outside. Rachel dragged her eyes from him and, determined to distract herself, took a moment to look around the room she'd landed in so inelegantly. The contrast between the front room and this kitchen couldn't be greater. From chaos, she'd stepped into a lifestyle magazine. Sunlight spilled in through wide windows with views out towards the bay, reflecting off the polished wooden worktops. A huge table, made of boards similar to the ones Leo was laying in the next room, occupied one half of the kitchen and an enormous range cooker occupied an inglenook fireplace. Glass doors opened out onto a small garden and a staircase wound up the wall in the corner of the room. It was beautiful, and when she looked at Leo it was with admiration for more than his well-developed lats.

He arrived back at the door to the kitchen with her case slung effortlessly over his shoulder. Okay, she was still admiring the lats, she realised, that perfect diagonal of muscle between underarm and waist—and reminded herself that all her future plans for her life came with a big fat *No Repeat Performance* clause. If she wanted to stay on track, she had to get her ogle under control.

'Luckily for you, the kitchen and bathrooms were finished first,' he said with a grin.

'This is beautiful.' She was still slightly taken aback by the contrast of this room with the building sites she'd seen so far, but determined to stay focused. 'Did you do all the work yourself?'

He nodded. 'Everything I legally can—an electrician did a couple of bits, but most of it was me.'

'You've done a great job.'

'Thanks.' He smiled and nodded, without false modesty or undue pride. 'Can I get you anything before I go and clean myself up? Coffee? Tea?' He glanced down at his sawdust-caked jeans and T-shirt as he spoke.

She brushed off his offer, instead getting him to point her towards coffee and mugs. When he'd disappeared up the stairs, Rachel turned to the cupboard and started on the coffee, almost squealing with delight when the tin next to the kettle turned out to contain cake and biscuits. Her eyes threatened to fill with tears—stupid hormones. But she guessed he wasn't the type to keep cake in the cupboard, and that meant it was only there for her sake. Butterflies were still causing havoc in her tummy, and she reluctantly admitted to herself that her nerves were more about the man, today, than the baby.

Once the initial gigantic I-don't-know-what-the-hell-is-going-to-happen-next panic had receded slightly, the day after she'd taken the pregnancy test, she'd started to think more and more about the baby growing inside her. About bringing a new life into the world, and excitement had grown and grown. Her thoughts about Leo? Still bound up with an almighty warning sign. And seeing his home, the centre of his disorder, hadn't helped. She rubbed her belly, thinking soothing thoughts, not wanting to inflict her worries on her baby. It seemed important already that she didn't allow her concerns to become his, or hers. Not as her parents had with her.

She turned as she heard Leo's footsteps on the stairs, and he appeared around the curve of the staircase in clean jeans and a black T-shirt, his hair a little damp.

'Sorry to abandon you like that. I looked in the mirror and thought I'd gone prematurely grey so I jumped in the shower to get rid of the dust.'

She smiled as she transferred coffee pot, mugs and cake to the table. 'And here was me thinking the shock had sent you all Marie Antoinette.'

He raised an eyebrow, questioning.

'Hair went white overnight? Never mind, obscure reference. Coffee and cake?'

'Sounds good,' Leo said, pulling out a chair and dropping into it. She watched his hands as he hacked a couple of wedges of cake, impressed and wondering whether she now had a pregnancy get-out clause when it came to denying her sweet tooth. She pulled up the chair beside him and poured the coffee, sending him sideways glances, wondering if he was finding this sudden domesticity as strange as she was. Bizarre, she thought. That she could find something so ordinary as coffee and cake new and nerve-racking when they were already somehow a family.

Rachel sipped the coffee and flinched when it scalded her lips. But it was worth it for the familiar caffeine buzz. The smell, even the taste, made her feel more comfortable. More herself. And the act of sitting at a great big table with a hot cup of coffee was all she needed to get her brain in gear, and have her reaching for her tablet. She grabbed her handbag, which she'd left propped by the chair, and pulled out all the plans she'd made since she'd first read *Pregnant* on that test. They had a lot to discuss, and it made sense to start work, she thought. She pulled herself up slightly on the word *work*; technically this was personal. But her—their—new life was going to take so much organising that it might as well be work. It was easier to think of it that way. To slot Leo and their child and all the changes they represented into her life as she would any other project. Because what was the alternative—chucking out everything she thought she knew and starting again?

But when she'd spread out her tablet and binders and looked up, she found Leo staring at her, a grimace on his face. She faltered slightly at the hard lines of his brows. The white knuckles of his fists.

'What are they?' The words were forced through his teeth, none too friendly. She glanced down—a little confused about how this had caused so much hostility. It wasn't as if he even knew what her plans contained. He'd gone white even at the thought of them.

'It's a tablet.' She spoke slowly, treading carefully in light of his sudden shift in mood. Not wanting to upset things further. 'And some charts. I had a few ideas about how we're going to make this work. I thought you might want to talk them through.'

'Oh, you did?' He took a long sip of his coffee—diversionary tactic, she guessed. 'And here was me thinking you were about to present me with a finished plan.' She dropped her eyes and felt her cheeks warm—it had never occurred to her to wait until she'd spoken to him before drawing up their options. But now they were laid out in front of her, and Leo was so obviously fighting to keep his annoyance under control, she could see that he was right.

'Did you just expect me to go along with everything you'd decided?'

Well, it wasn't as if he'd made any suggestions—it had been all down to her.

But when could he have contributed? She'd not seen him since they'd found out the news; she hadn't given him a chance. 'I'm sorry. I should have spoken to you first.' Her plans were good, though, thorough. They covered myriad scenarios with timetables, budgets and schedules. And of course Leo had a say. But *she* was the one carrying the baby. *She* was the one who would have to take time off for the birth. *She* was the one who would have to decide whether, and how, she could return to work.

She was the one who would have to put what little she recognised of her life back together after the baby was born.

And it wasn't as if she hadn't considered what Leo wanted. She'd given him plenty of options, with his involvement ranging from full-time parenting to 'financial contribution only'. Even—though nothing she'd seen of Leo so far told her that she'd need it—a 'no involve-ment' plan.

'I thought we were going to have a coffee.' Leo's tone was still harsh, and he gripped his mug as if struggling to keep his temper.

'Can't we drink and talk?'

'Sure, we can drink and talk. But that's not what you're suggesting. You want to drink and *work*.'

He was beyond tense now, and heading di-rectly for angry. His body language was defen-sive, closed, and she could see from the lines of fear on his face that she'd stumbled into deeper waters than she'd thought. He wasn't just angry at her for doing this without him. Her temper had lit in response to his, but she forced it down, trying to keep neutral. Trying to understand what had him so wary. If she blew up, too, they'd never talk this through.

'We don't have to do this all today. But I'd

like to make a start, if we can. We've got quite a lot to get through—'

'Get through?' He slammed his mug onto the table, and hot coffee spilled onto the wood, creeping towards her papers. She pulled them back, eyeing Leo, suddenly realising she'd completely underestimated how badly she'd read him, how much distance there was between them. How impossible it was going to be to create a family out of this mess. 'I'm not a project, Rachel. I'm not a client or a boss or someone you're giving a presentation to. This isn't going to be solved over a working lunch and a follow-up email.'

'But—'

'No!'

Rachel set her cup down slowly, willing herself to remain calm in the face of his raw emotion, wishing she could understand what was making him react this way. She hadn't expected this to be *easy*, but she hadn't expected such vehement opposition, either. She shut her eyes and counted to ten, hoping that when she opened them again Leo would've lost the frightened, cornered, *angry* look that twisted his features—usually so effortlessly sexy—into something ugly.

She looked up. He had calmed a little, the redness draining from his face, but there were still deep creases between his brows, and his mouth was set in a harsh line.

'I'm sorry, but I cannot have your plan dictated to me and just go along with it.' The clipped consonants and snappy vowels gave away the effort that near-civility was costing him. 'I know you need this. I know you want everything decided, booked, settled. But it's not just you now. Can't you see that?' He could see it, and he didn't know how to get away from it. 'If we decide something, we have to do it *together*. I will not let you plan and schedule and itemise my life just because I happened to get you pregnant. That doesn't give you the right to come in here and tell me how it's going to be.'

'I've given you choices…options.' Finally she couldn't keep the anger from her own voice. With the venom contained in his, it didn't seem optional—it was a necessity. A way to fend off his biting accusations.

'You don't get to *give* me anything. That's not how *together* works.'

'What's made you so scared?' she asked. 'Tell me why my having a plan freaks you out. Because as far as I can see, with us barely knowing each other, and living hours apart, and having an actual *baby* together, some idea of how we're going to cope seems like a good idea. So why is it you blanch, pretty much start shaking and bite my head off?'

He scraped his chair backwards, leaving a good couple of feet between him and the table, the space acting like a force field around him. 'I can't do it like this, Rachel. I won't. I can't sit here, backed into a corner with no way out of what you've decided for us. I won't be trapped.'

And with that he headed straight out of the door, leaving her sitting at the kitchen table wondering what the hell had just happened. Her heart was hammering in her chest, tears pricked at her eyes, and her fingers shook slightly when she reached for a cloth to mop up the spilled coffee.

How had they got here? They'd gone from almost kissing when she'd arrived to the point where they couldn't be in the same room together.

And now she was scared—because nothing he had said or done made her believe that he was in any way glad about the fact they were having a baby. In the days since she'd found out she was expecting, she'd started to look forward to being a parent. Feel joy at the prospect of meeting the new life they had created. Of course there was an enormous dose of full-body-paralysis fear, not least when she tried to think about how she could possibly spend the next eighteen—or eighty—years trying to maintain some sort of contact with Leo.

The thought of having to live with the disorder and randomness that Leo so clearly needed threatened to bring on another panic attack. But when he had headed for the door just now, her stomach had dropped and her heart had felt as if it had stopped. She had been filled with an overwhelming dread that he might not come back. That he was leaving her to have this baby alone. She knew that she could do it if she had to. But in the second that she thought that Leo might be walking away, she wanted him by her side. Chaos and all. They had made this new life together, and she wanted to find a way for them to be a family.

She cleared away a few pieces from the table—for no reason other than that she didn't want to be just sitting waiting for him when he got back. So when she heard his footsteps at the door, she had her back to him, running something under the tap and holding her breath.

'I'm sorry,' he said eventually, in a shaky voice redolent of raw emotion.

She stared into the sink a little longer, gathering her thoughts, and fighting down the swell of tears that seemed to be climbing her throat. She couldn't account for them, couldn't reason why the croak of his voice made hers swell with sympathy.

'I'm sorry, too.' She turned off the tap and slumped back against the sink, relief washing through her. 'I shouldn't have made those plans without you.'

'And I shouldn't have snapped at you like that. I'm genuinely sorry. But there are some things we need to talk about if we're going to make this work. I know you like to have everything all worked out, but I can't do that.'

'So what am I meant to do? Just wait and see if you turn up at my office again?' She tried to laugh, to pretend she could live like that, but it sounded hollow even to her.

'Would that be so bad? I'd make sure I was there when you—when the baby—needed me. Does everything need to be planned months in advance?'

Her spine straightened again; Leo's presence was seemingly anathema to serenity. 'And is that what I should tell my doctor? Oh, I'll definitely come along at some point. An appointment? No. I'll just arrive when I'm ready.'

'And what about the baby—is he allowed to arrive when he's ready, or are you going to hold him to whatever due date the doctors pull out of the air? I hope for his sake he isn't late.'

She was about to snap back, when her train

of thought faltered and her voice failed. 'Wait, he?' she asked, with the beginnings of a smile tweaking her lips. 'Who says it's a boy?'

His face softened, and for the first time she saw the hard expression around his eyes ease, and his usual humorous glint return. She found she was relieved to see it, had been worried for a few moments that she and the baby had caused its disappearance to become permanent. It had been his determination to make her laugh that had drawn them together that first night, and she was worried that without that humour between them the very foundations they were working on were unsteady.

'I don't know. In my head, when I think about how things will be, I just always see a boy.'

'You've thought about it?'

His eyes bugged.

'Have I thought about it? What else am I meant to think about? Have you thought about anything else?'

'No,' she admitted. 'So what do you?'

He raised an eyebrow by way of a question. 'What do I…?'

'What do you think, when you think about it?'

He crossed to the table and dropped into a seat, reaching for his abandoned cup of coffee.

A smile was creeping across her face at the sight of the hint of a grin on his. He thought about their baby. The knowledge glowed inside her. 'I don't know. Just flashes of things, I suppose.'

'Good things?'

'Mostly.' They shared a long look, mutual happiness turning both their mouths up like a mirror. But they couldn't leave it there. If they wanted this to work, they had to dig deeper than that. Learn to trust one another.

'And the bad?' she asked.

'This.' He motioned towards her colour-coded papers. 'This is pretty much every bad thing I've imagined since Wednesday afternoon. I want you to know, Rachel, that I'm here for you and for the baby. But I will not do this entirely on your terms. We're *both* going to have to compromise.'

'And the first thing that's got to go is any attempt at a plan?' She couldn't help her defensiveness—he was threatening the only thing that was keeping her in any way connected to sanity.

'This plan? Yes. We didn't discuss a single thing before you made it. Of course it has to go.'

She felt a wave of nausea as she realised what he was saying. Every plan she had made in the past few days. All the words and the numbers and the tidy tick-boxes that had soothed her mind—were going to be thrown out. Already panic was making the edges of her thoughts fuzzy, and that wave of nausea was starting to feel more like a tsunami. With a shock, she realised it was more than just nausea. She must have looked pretty green, because as her hand flew to her mouth Leo was already by her side, grabbing her free hand and pulling her to the stairs.

CHAPTER FIVE

LEO LEANED AGAINST the landing wall, trying not to hear the noises emanating from the bathroom, and wondering whether he was relieved or annoyed that Rachel had so easily brushed away his offer of help and slammed the bathroom door shut with him on the outside. Not that it sounded a particularly appealing place to be right now, but the knowledge that she was perfectly happy doing this alone—was happier doing it alone—made his chest uncomfortable. Because at the moment, it felt as if any involvement in his child's life depended entirely on this woman's opinion of him, and was entirely on her terms. He'd been terrified, was still terrified, when she'd told him that she was pregnant; but the thought of his child out there in the world not even knowing him was more frightening still.

He'd have to apologise for snapping at her like that. Losing his cool definitely didn't help him get what he needed—but he had to get her to see his point, and to agree with it. Of course there were parts of this situation that he couldn't avoid planning in advance—he was perfectly prepared to understand that a doctor's appointment had to be made for a particular time. And though the thought of those appointments stretching out for years in the future didn't do brilliant things to him, it didn't fill him with the same queasy dread he'd felt when he'd glimpsed the plan she'd drawn up. Just the headings told him he was in trouble. Timing. Finance. Schooling. *Schooling?* He didn't even know when the baby was due, and they were talking schooling already? Did she even know yet when it was due? Had she been to the doctor? Probably things he would know already if he hadn't walked out on her. The bathroom had gone quiet, and he leaned back against the door.

'Rachel?' he shouted through the wood. 'All okay in there?'

'Fine,' she replied and he could hear tears in her voice. Was that the sickness or something else?

'Can I get you anything?'

'No, I'm fine. I just need to catch my breath.' He heard her lean back against the door, and he followed her down, until the old oak was supporting them both.

'Then can I ask you a question?'

He took the mumble he could hear as a yes.

'Tell me about the plans. Why do you need them? Help me understand.'

He held his breath, hoping that she would trust him. See that he was reaching out to her, and wanting her to reach back. He needed to understand her. To try and find out how they were going to manage to get along, now that they were tied together.

'I don't need them. I just like to have an idea of what's going on. What's wrong with that?'

'There'd be nothing wrong with that. But that's not how you felt downstairs just now, was it?'

He listened through the door, wishing he could see her face, wishing he could at least see her expression. Just as he was giving up hope that she would ever speak…

'It makes me feel safe.'

He was almost tempted to laugh at that, the quirk of fate that had brought him together with a woman who could only feel safe if he felt bone-chillingly terrified. Instead he heard the trepidation in her voice, the hint of tears. He wanted to break down the door, wrap his arms around her and tell her that they would be okay. Or, failing that, tease and kiss her until the tension left her shoulders, until her limbs were heavy and languid, wrapped around him. Instead, he asked another question, hoping that the pain now would be worth it eventually.

'Why?'

He pressed his head back against the solid wood of the door, wondering if she could feel how close he was. Whether she wanted him closer, the way he wanted her.

The memories of the night they had spent together had often played on his mind in the weeks after. Flashbacks, scents, snatches of songs all reminded him of the hours they'd spent wrapped around each other. And he couldn't deny that these memories had something to do with why he'd been so keen to meet with Will and discuss the idea he'd had—to create a sculpture for the Julia House charity. They could keep it in the grounds, or auction it for money. Whatever they thought would benefit their patients most. He'd floated a couple of ideas to Will the night of the fundraiser— always with half an eye for whether Will's assistant would take an interest in the conversation.

Then after he'd left Rachel at the station, the momentary relief he'd felt as his train had pulled away had faded quickly, leaving him dissatisfied, feeling as if he'd missed an opportunity. Maybe he'd been too hasty running from her then, he'd thought as he'd made the phone call to Will. Maybe they could have had a few more nights like the previous one before they inevitably went their separate ways. As he'd taken the train up to London, he'd let himself imagine how she'd react to seeing him again. And then a little longer thinking of everything they could get up to if she was of the same mind.

The shock of a baby in the works had seemingly done nothing to quell his fierce imagination.

He jumped up at the turning of the lock and was brushing off his jeans when the door opened and Rachel appeared, looking a little pale. 'Morning sickness, I guess,' she said as she walked out. He nodded as if he understood, but beyond the fact that he knew pregnant women were sick sometimes he was pretty much clueless. For a start, shouldn't it happen in the morning? He didn't know the exact time—he hadn't worn a watch since he was a kid. It was probably past eleven when he left his workshop. And he'd laid floorboards and half carried a pregnant woman up a flight of stairs since then. It was definitely well past morning.

'Sorry, it took me by surprise. It's not happened before,' she continued, as clipped and professional as if he'd called by her office. He stopped her with a hand on her shoulder and gently turned her face up to him.

'I borrowed your toothbrush,' she blurted, and he guessed from the rosy blush of her cheeks she'd not meant to confess. He laughed, the re-emergence of her human side relaxing him.

'No worries.' He smiled at her. 'I think we're a little past worrying about a shared toothbrush.' He was gratified by her small smile, but a little uneasy at how his own insides relaxed at the sight of it.

'So what now?' she asked as they hovered on the landing. She looked lost, smaller somehow, as if she was losing a grip on what it was that allowed her to present her usual polished, professional, vibrant face to the world. He knew what she was missing—her plan— but he couldn't bring himself to look at it yet. Not even for her. But he could offer her a distraction, a plan for the next hour or so. He hoped it would be enough.

'What about a walk on the beach? An ice cream and fish and chips—if you're hungry.'

She nodded and he remembered the night they met, when he'd heard the clear chime of her laugh and seen it as a challenge to get her to make that sound as many times as he could. The prospect seemed a distant one right now. But he'd made a connection with her before. Felt her relax in his arms. If they could do that again, find the connection that had strung between them that night and held strong until the next morning.

'A walk and an ice cream,' she repeated. 'I think I can manage that. I just need to change. Where…?' She glanced around the landing and he felt a stirring heat inside him. He wanted to curse the gentlemanly instinct that had made him tell her that he had a spare room, and had him working through the night for the past couple of days to get it ready for her. Even if it meant that he was sleeping on a mattress on bare floorboards.

He shook away the tempting image of sharing a room with her, and concentrated on their maintaining civility for the time being. That they couldn't even make it through a cup of coffee without fighting had shown him all too clearly how fragile this relationship was—how easily it could fall apart around them. He'd had no ulterior motive in inviting Rachel to come and stay. He really did want to get to know her better. Now he was starting to realise that he'd been hoping to get her to do things his way.

To show her his way of life and hope that she would want it. This had shown him how precarious their situation was.

He pushed open the door to the guest room and stood back to let her past him. 'This is yours,' he said, even as he was turning away. He tried to brush past her—suddenly unable to think of being alone in a bedroom with her, and cursed the narrow doorway as he found himself pressed against her. He dropped his hands to her hips as he attempted to get by, but kept his eyes on their feet—determined not to be drawn in, not yet.

But the press of her body was electric against his, and her hair beneath his face smelt fresh and fruity. On impulse he lifted a lock of it, twisting it around his fingers. Rachel's eyes snapped up to his, and for a long moment their gazes held. All sensible considerations threatened to fall away in the onslaught of her body on his senses. But he couldn't give in to it. Couldn't lose sight of all the reasons getting any more involved with her was an impossibility. Dropping her hair, and pulling his eyes away, he jogged down the stairs and leaned back against the wall as he reached the kitchen. It was starting to look as if his bright idea had been a huge mistake.

He returned upstairs with her suitcase and

a glass of water. Reaching out to knock on the open door, he caught sight of Rachel, silhouetted by the window, looking out over the water. The light was catching her hair, highlighting every shade of chocolate and chestnut, and a subtle smile turned the corners of her lips. She looked almost dreamy, and at that moment he would have given just about anything to know what she was thinking. But his foot hit a creaky floorboard, and she turned around, her relaxed expression replaced by something more guarded.

'This is beautiful,' she said, glancing round the room as she took in the furniture he'd found, sanded, painted and waxed. The light he'd sculpted from a block of driftwood, and the seascapes painted by a local artist friend, mounted in frames he'd made in his workshop. But her eyes hovered on the evidence of his labour only briefly. Because they were drawn inexorably to the window, and out over the water. The window itself was an exercise in love and commitment. The product of arguments with planning authorities, and then wrestling with metres-long expanses of timber and glass, all to create this huge, unbroken picture of the sea. It was calm today, just a few white-crested waves breaking up the expanse of ever-shifting blue-green.

If he'd known beforehand, though, what it would have taken to get the thing finished—the hearings and the plans, and the revised plans and rescheduled hearings—he wasn't sure that he could have started.

He handed Rachel the glass of water, and his gaze rested on her face rather than being drawn out to sea. Her eyelashes were long and soft, and brushed the skin beneath her eyes when she blinked. There were faint shadows there, he realised. He wondered whether they were new, or whether he'd just not seen them before. But he was struck by a protective instinct, the desire to look after her, ensure she was sleeping. Her hair had been pulled back into a loose tail—a style that owed more to her morning sickness than anything else, he guessed. The navy dress she wore wouldn't have been out of place among the stiff suits at her office. His eyes finally dropped to her belly—still as flat as he remembered it, but where her child, *their* child, was growing. It seemed almost impossible that a whole life could be growing with no outward sign.

She turned, and must have caught the direction of his gaze, because her hands dropped to her tummy. She spread her fingers and palms, stretching the fabric flat against her, and then looked up and caught his eye.

'Nothing to see yet,' she said with a small, cautious smile. 'It'll be a couple more months before I start to show.' He nodded again, as if he had the faintest clue about any of this. As if at the sight of her hands on her belly he wasn't remembering the last time he'd seen her fingers spread across her skin like that. He held her gaze, wondering if she remembered, too. But she gave a little start, pulling back her shoulders and straightening her posture— leaving him in no way uncertain that if she was remembering, she wasn't too happy about it.

'I'll see you downstairs,' he said, giving her the space her expression told him she needed.

CHAPTER SIX

AS THEY STROLLED along the beach, Rachel felt the tension of the past few hours draining from her limbs, being replaced by the gentle warm glow of summer sunshine. They'd walked down the coastal path from the cottage, barely exchanging a word, but somehow the silence felt companionable, rather than awkward. She was taken aback, as she had been at the window upstairs, by the beauty of Leo's home. It perched on a cliff above the beach, and even with the tarpaulin for a roof, and the building materials dumped in the yard, the way it nestled into the rock and sand, shutters on the outside of the window, even the way the front door reflected the colour of the sea all helped it look as if it were a natural part of the landscape, as if it had emerged from the Jurassic rocks fully formed and—almost—habitable.

With the sun warming her hair, and the gentle exercise distracting her from the slight queasiness still troubling her stomach, she reached a decision. They were never going to be able to be friends if they didn't understand each other. Leo had asked her a question, one she'd avoided answering up till now, but he wanted to know why she needed a plan so badly, and if she was to stand any chance of him cooperating with it, then she at least had to expect to tell him why.

'You asked me why I need a plan,' she said, as they stopped momentarily to step over a pool of spray that had gathered on the rocks.

'To feel safe, you said.'

She nodded, wondering how she could explain, where to start.

'When I was fourteen, my parents left me home alone while they went out. It wasn't anything special, just cinema and dinner, I think. I'd gone to bed, but woke up when I heard a noise from my dad's study. I went downstairs and disturbed a burglar.'

Leo had stopped on the sand, and turned to face her. 'I'm so sorry,' he said, his face lined with genuine concern. 'That must have been awful for you.'

'I got a nasty bump to the head—he lashed out as he tried to get away—but I recovered pretty quickly. Not that you would have believed that if you'd listened to my parents.'

She dropped to her bottom in the sand, shielding her eyes from the sun and looking out over the water.

'They blamed themselves,' she explained. 'Thought that they never should have left me, that I'd been in huge amounts of danger and that I'd been lucky to survive.'

'They must have been so relieved that you hadn't been more seriously hurt.'

She shook her head, trying not to get drawn back into the suffocating anxiety her parents had forced on her.

'It never felt that way. They spent so much time concentrating on all the terrible things that could have happened, it got harder and harder to remember.' She fell quiet as she watched the waves, and glanced up a couple of times, following the path of the seagulls above the water. The sand was warm beneath her thighs, and she turned her face to the sun, letting the rays soak into her skin. Because she'd still not got to the difficult bit.

It had never occurred to her before that her planning might be a problem. That her need to know when and how the events in her life would unfold had become something that held her back, rather than helped her. It wasn't until she'd seen the revulsion in Leo's face when he'd glimpsed her plan that she'd realised how others might see her, how far from 'normal' her life had become. But it didn't really matter what anyone else thought about it. Even when that person was the father of her child, because she didn't know how to live any differently.

'I understand it must have been a difficult time…' Leo had dropped to the sand beside her, looking out over the water, as she was, so she didn't have to worry about his intensely blue eyes following every emotion that fluttered across her face. She wanted him to understand, because she wanted, needed, them to be friends. So she fought away the instinct to hide what had happened next, to protect herself and her family, by skirting around the behaviour that had locked them all into their fears.

'It was, but what happened next was harder.' It was the first time she'd admitted that. That the love and care that her parents had shown her in the weeks after the burglary had been more difficult to cope with than the initial trauma.

'My parents wouldn't let me out of the house.' She really hadn't meant for that to sound so dramatic. And she knew from the way that Leo had turned sharply to look at her that he'd misunderstood. 'They didn't lock me in or anything,' she clarified quickly, imagining a bevy of policemen or social workers or other officials turning up on her parents' doorstep and accusing them of crimes they'd never committed. 'They were just worried about me, and they liked to know where I was. They became anxious if I was out of the house too long, so I was never allowed to friends' houses or after-school clubs—I didn't really have any hobbies outside of home.'

'I still don't see what this has to do with the plan you presented this morning,' Leo said. His voice was soft, and his hand twitched in the sand, as if he wanted to reach for her. For a moment, she wished that he would. That he would thread his fingers with hers. Somehow she thought that it might be easier, to draw on his strength, to face her past together. Ridiculous, she told herself. They had only known each other a few weeks. Had really spent only a few waking hours together. There was no reason she should feel stronger just for having him there. But she couldn't deny how that twitch of his hand had affected her, how much she wished for the contact.

'I'll get to it, I will. It's just all tied up with everything else. I don't know how to tell you *just* that, if you see what I mean.' She turned to look at him and he nodded. 'I was still in school, they at least thought that I could be safe there, but I could see how much I was missing. I was losing touch with my friends, having to go straight home every night while they were meeting in parks and shopping centres and fast-food places. I was lonely, and I knew that things couldn't carry on as they were, with me speaking to no one outside school but my parents. So I negotiated a system. I would be allowed out with my classmates and friends if I provided my parents with a schedule of where I would be and when. They would have the landline numbers of anywhere I would be so that they could call and check I was really there. I had a mobile as well, of course, so that they could always get hold of me.

'If I was going out at the weekend, I'd plot out exactly what I'd be doing and when, give the itinerary to my parents, and then stick to it like my life depended on it. If they called and I wasn't where I was supposed to be, I knew that all hell could break loose. It wasn't just that they'd ground me—I knew that they would be terrified. And much as I didn't agree with the way they were wrapping me in cotton wool, I knew that they were only doing it because they loved me. Everything they did was because they were terrified of me getting hurt and they only wanted the best for me. I would never do anything that would upset them. They'd been through enough. Or felt that they had, at least. I didn't want to add to it.'

'So how long did it take?'

She looked at Leo in confusion.

'How long did what take?'

'Until it rubbed off. Until you started to believe that the schedule kept you safe, the same way your parents did.'

She started a little, surprised that he'd understood so clearly.

'Well, my friends all thought it was a little odd, that I had to be where I had to be and exactly on time. But when I was living at home, it wasn't easy to see where my parents' need ended and mine started. It wasn't until I went to university full of ideas of living on the edge, of being spontaneous and pleasing no one but myself, that I realised that I needed the schedule as much as they had.'

'Leaving home. I guess that was hard on you all.'

'It was. Painfully so. I had no idea before I left just how hard it would be. I'd known all along that it would be for them. But I could also see how strong the apron strings were, how they would get harder to break as I got older. So I managed to convince them that I had to have a normal life. And I was eighteen—there was nothing much they could do about it anyway. I think perhaps they worried that if they didn't let me go, I'd take myself off and they might lose contact with me. If I went with their blessing, I was more likely to keep in touch.'

'So how was it?' Leo's voice was still low, gentle, but probing. Encouraging her to share, leaving her nowhere to hide her secrets.

She let out a long, slow breath as she remembered those first few weeks, when she'd clung to her class schedule and the fresher's week itinerary as if they were a lifeline.

'Hard. Really hard. I didn't know anyone, and my teen years had been pretty sheltered. The only way I knew how to cope with the confusion, the novelty of it all, was to make a plan and stick to it. So I mapped out the weeks and the months. Looked ahead to the career that I wanted and the life that I wanted, and started filling in the days in my calendar. Fast forward a decade or so, and here I am, right on track. Or was, until…'

'Until you met me.'

She nodded, but something about the familiar intimacy in his voice, the hint of remembered laughter, made her smile.

'So your first instinct was to make a new plan. You need it.'

'I…I do,' she admitted. 'It seemed the only way to make sense of this whole situation. But seeing it through your eyes, it's clear I need it a little too much, that there are times when going with the flow or being more flexible can have their place. But it's not something I can just turn off. And trust me, I've never felt more like I need a plan than I have this week.'

'So we'll work something out together. Enough of a plan for you to feel comfortable and enough flexibility that it doesn't feel like a prison to me.' His voice sounded rough, low, and she looked up to catch the concern on his face, mixed with a distance she hadn't felt from him before. He shook his head, and when he looked back at her his expression was lighter, sunnier.

'When do we start?'

He laughed, and leant back on his arms, one of them nudging slightly behind her back. 'How about not right this minute? If we say we'll make a start today, is that enough of a plan for now?'

'It'll do.' She grinned.

'Good, because I'm starving, and I'm guessing after your spell in the bathroom you could use a big portion of fish and chips. What do you say?'

'I say you're a mind-reader. Where's good?'

Leo pushed to his feet and reached down to help her up. As she felt her hand disappear between his huge, roughened palms, her body shuddered. Pulled to her feet, she realised that—without her heels—Leo towered over her. He'd pulled her up to him, and now she was probably standing a little too close. She should take a step back, she thought. But seeing Leo here, there was something hypnotising about it. Until now, she'd only ever seen him in her world: her party, her flat, her work. Here, by his home, surrounded by the beach and the sea that he loved so much, it added an extra dimension of sexy. It brought out the gold shining in his hair, made his slightly windchapped cheeks more attractive, like a good wine bringing out the flavours in food.

The wind had caught her hair, and was playing it around her temples, tickling at her face. She was reaching up to tame it when Leo caught it and tucked it behind her ear. His hand rested there, and for a moment Rachel was more than tempted to turn her face into his palm, to press her skin against his, to refind the pleasure of that night. But she held her breath and stepped away. There was too much at risk; she could get too hurt. They needed to be friends and there was no surer way to ruin a friendship than a disastrous romance.

His eyes lingered on hers for a moment as she moved back, and his expression told her he knew exactly what she had felt between them just now, told her exactly what had been on offer, had she wanted it. And that he knew she'd deliberately stepped back from it.

CHAPTER SEVEN

LEO SAT LISTENING to the kettle coming to the boil, wondering whether he should wake Rachel. After a long walk down the beach yesterday afternoon, and a portion of fish and chips for dinner, she'd crashed almost as soon as they'd arrived back at the house. And had been asleep more than twelve hours. He wondered whether she'd been working too hard. Weren't pregnant women meant to take things easy? Perhaps she'd been overdoing it. Should he say something?

But what right did he have to even ask her that? Did the fact that she was carrying his child give him a right to question what she was doing? He shook his head. There were still so many things they hadn't discussed. But discussing meant deciding. And deciding meant getting it in writing, laminating and deviating only on the point of death.

He made a coffee and decided to leave her.

She'd wake when she was ready. And maybe he could subtly ask her later whether she thought she should be taking things easier. He really needed to know more about pregnancy, about *babies*. He'd never given any thought to starting a family; it had always seemed a distant, uncertain thing. And he'd never imagined he'd be facing it with someone he barely knew. Perhaps he could ask his mum these questions. He'd have to tell her. And his dad, too.

He gave a shudder as he acknowledged what he'd been trying to ignore since he'd first found out about the baby. He'd have to see his family. His brother. He'd avoided him for years, had barely seen him since he'd left school. He knew that he was hurting his parents, that they despaired of ever seeing their family all together again. But what else could he do—sit down to a happy family dinner with him? The man who had made his life miserable—who had led the school bullies. So miserable that when he'd left school, escaped them, he'd sworn that he'd never again find himself in a situation he didn't like without an escape route. Which was why the news that Rachel was pregnant had terrified him. Because if there was any situation more impossible to escape than this one, he didn't want to know about it.

She would want to make a start on that plan

this morning. Even when she'd been falling-over tired last night she'd mentioned wanting to do it. It was only the interruption of an enormous yawn that had made her listen to him and finally take herself off to bed—and a promise that they could talk about it today.

He only knew one thing for certain—no child of his would be subjected to the experience he'd had. He wanted a better life for him, or her.

What were the other headings in Rachel's magnum opus? Finance? She obviously knew—or thought she knew—that he was well off. After all, he'd made the generous donation she'd not so subtly hinted at the night of the fundraiser. But that was family money, not his. He'd always been happy to send his trust-fund proceeds the way of those who really needed them—but had never used it for himself.

He'd seen the damage done when people inherited money without responsibility. Stick a load of those with an inflated sense of self-worth together, with insufficient supervision, and you had a recipe for disaster—and emotional torture in his case. If Rachel thought that she'd found herself a meal ticket she would be sadly disappointed. But he didn't really think that was what she was interested in.

Creaking floorboards upstairs told him that

she was awake. He gave a start, half pleased at the thought of seeing her, half dreading the discussion he knew would inevitably come. Remembering the hour she'd spent in the bathroom the night he'd stayed at her flat, he expected a little more grace before he had to face her, but then he heard her footsteps on the stairs.

For half a second, he wondered if he'd be treated to the sight of her in some sort of skimpy nightwear. The sight of her perfectly prim jeans and soft sweater reminded him she'd come here prepared for a business meeting. At least she wasn't clutching her tablet. In fact, he couldn't even see her phone on her. Though looking for it gave him a brilliant excuse for thoroughly checking out the pockets of her jeans.

'Morning,' he said, standing up from the table. Once he was on his feet, he wasn't sure why he had done it, except that it seemed impossible not to react to her, not to want to get close. 'Can I get you anything?'

He bit his tongue to stop the flood of questions filling his mouth. She had more colour in her cheeks than she had the previous afternoon, but he was still worried. As he reached her side, he rested a gentle hand on her shoulder, turning her to face him. 'Did you sleep well?' he asked, looking for any sign that she wasn't completely recovered from yesterday. An overwhelming need to protect her swept over him, and the hand on her shoulder slipped to her waist, pulling her closer. Once her body was near enough that he felt her magnetic pull, all thoughts of protecting her flew out of his mind, and were replaced with something hotter, more urgent. He pulled the arm around her waist tight, and dipped his head. His eyes were already closing as his body remembered the feel of hers, as his lips tingled with remembered sensation.

And then he was cold, his body left bereft as Rachel turned and pulled away until his arms were empty.

'I'll make the coffee,' she said, the shake in her voice at least showing that she wasn't completely immune to him. 'And I could murder some carbs. What is there for breakfast?'

He pulled his brain back to the real world, the one where they weren't a lust-filled couple shacked up together for a fun weekend. To the world where an ill-thought-through night had led to a baby, a lifetime of commitment, and he was momentarily glad that her self-control had outwitted his libido. 'Toast? Cereal?' He tried to keep his voice level, to take her cue and pretend that his clumsy attempt at a kiss hadn't happened. But he couldn't forget it, couldn't forget how it felt to be fractions of a second from bliss, and then left cold and wanting her.

She nodded, her body stiff, her smile a little forced. He threw bread into the toaster, dug around in the cupboard and put together a carb-loaded platter: muffins, crumpets, toast and cereal, anything to keep mind and body busy and away from her. They feasted on the breads, slathered in honey and jam, and conversation eventually started to flow between them almost as smooth.

He remembered the challenge he'd set himself that night. The way the sound of her laugh had so entranced him he was determined to make it happen again and again. The effect hadn't worn off. Every smile and chuckle became a challenge to make it grow. He felt himself relax as she slouched a little more in her chair, as her words flowed easy and her smiles grew. Every chime of her laughter swelled a light in his chest, something primal and basic, something he couldn't control, or make himself want to.

As they finished up with breakfast, he was tempted to hold his breath, to hold on to these moments of happiness, because something told him that this was borrowed contentment. That it wasn't real. Maybe this was in her plan all along, softening him up before she started. No need to spook him by hitting him with talk about the plan the minute she was up. Instead she lulled him into a false sense of security, waiting until he entered a food coma until she made her move. With the prospect of having to make some sort of plan on the horizon, he couldn't see what was real and what was his fear manifesting as paranoia.

She was fidgeting as they cleared the table, clearly getting more and more uncomfortable. There was tension in her shoulders and a tightness in her muscles that he didn't like. And he knew the only thing that would get rid of it. She was still flailing after he'd ripped up her plan. Writing a new one would ease her worries, make her feel safe.

Of course he'd discovered one other way of finding the relaxed, happy, free Rachel. And he knew which of the two—drawing up a schedule for the rest of his life, or a long, languorous morning of lovemaking—he would prefer.

But he also knew which of the two Rachel needed today. So he swallowed the very tempting suggestion and did what he hoped was the right thing. 'I think we should take a look at this plan.' He ran his hands through his hair and left them at the back of his head. He supposed he was hoping for 'oh, we don't have to do that now,' or, 'maybe we could leave it for a bit'. Though of course what he actually got was a sigh of relief, a smile and darting glances at the stairs. 'Grab whatever you need,' he said, suddenly feeling distant and uncomfortable around her, with her need for control—and his fear of it—sitting between them like a threat. 'I'll make some more coffee.'

She hesitated at the bottom of the stairs. 'Do you have any decaf?'

'Sorry, I didn't think.'

He leaned back against the kitchen counter as she went upstairs. Decaf? Another pregnancy thing, he assumed. Just one more part of this whole situation he was completely clueless about. Every good feeling he'd had when they'd shared breakfast had abandoned him, and even the house seemed darker and colder this side of the meal. Rachel re-emerged from the stairs a few moments later, clutching her bound-up papers, a notebook and her tablet.

'Old-fashioned or new-fangled?' she asked as she sat neatly at the table and set everything out in front of her. Death by fire or water? What did it matter?

But the smile had returned to her lips, her arms hung loosely at her sides, and she had lost the drawn, haunted look that told of a frightened woman.

'You choose.' He tried to keep the weighty, quavery feeling fluttering in his belly out of his voice. 'You're the expert here.' He hoped it didn't sound snarky. He didn't mean it to. Didn't mean to blame her for how uncomfortable he was. It didn't make sense to be angry at her for the situation they found themselves in. It wasn't her fault they were pregnant. It wasn't her fault that the way she wanted to live her life was the opposite of his. They just had to find a way to make this work for both of them. All of them.

'Old-fashioned, then.' She opened the notebook out to a blank double spread and reached for her pen. He could tell she was itching to write her headings across the top of the page but seemed to be waiting for his okay to do so. 'So…where do you want to start?'

He took a deep breath. She'd obviously spent a lot of time thinking about this. And to be honest her plan was probably as good as anything that they could come up with together. As he'd said—she was the expert here. But if he didn't have his say now, then when would he? Would he find himself in ten years' time on a path that she had chosen, and that he had never had any idea of where it was going? If he didn't rein this in, if she couldn't learn to live a little less rigidly, he'd find himself stifled and trapped. And if she couldn't start compromising now, then he couldn't see how this was ever going to work.

'Perhaps we could start with the next few weeks,' he said eventually, thinking that even he could manage with planning that far out, if he had to. 'And anything that needs a specific date. Appointments, travel plans, that sort of thing.'

Rachel nodded and he could tell from the small smile on her face she already knew exactly how she expected the next few weeks to pan out. She probably had appointments lined up, time blocked out, and knew exactly where he should be and at what time. But she said none of this and instead waited for him to make a suggestion. At least she seemed willing to try as hard as he was to make this work.

'Do you have any doctor's appointments scheduled? I'm not really sure how this works but I'd like to be there if that's what you want.'

'I've an appointment with my GP in a few days. Probably won't be much to tell at that stage, from what I've read. But generally they want to schedule the first scan at some point around twelve weeks.'

'Twelve weeks?' He raised a brow in question.

'The twelfth week of the pregnancy. Not

twelve weeks from now. Or, in fact, twelve weeks from when we…' He smiled a little at her embarrassment. 'The counting is weird,' she continued, a light blush colouring her cheeks. 'Right now I think I'm about nine weeks pregnant, even though it's not that long since we… They count from the first day of your last…'

'Are you going to finish a sentence today?' He laughed at the sudden appearance of this bashfulness. 'Or is there always going to be so much guesswork?'

'I'm sorry. It seems stupid to be embarrassed talking about any of this when you're the one, well, we're the ones… Sorry.'

She laughed, too, and Leo relaxed into his chair as the tension in the air palpably lightened. What was it about her laugh that reached his spine and his heart?

'I'm doing it again, aren't I?' He nodded. 'They count from the first day of your last period, which means today is week nine of the pregnancy even though it's not been that long since we…met. Which means they'll want to schedule the scan for around three weeks' time.'

'I'd like to be there.'

'Me, too.' They both smiled, and he breathed a sigh of relief, glad that they'd found this common ground at last. Maybe they *could* do this. Maybe they could find a compromise to make them both happy. And if they did that, what next? What more could there be between them when they weren't both terrified of what the other craved?

Rachel drew a column on the piece of paper and wrote the heading *Appointments* at the top; then clicked through the screen of her phone with one hand and wrote the date in the column with the other. She glanced up at him. 'Do you want to make a note of the date?'

Or maybe they couldn't. 'What date? You haven't got an appointment yet.'

'No, but I'm sure they'll make it that week. You could…'

'Rachel, this is one of those times when you're going to have to let me make a decision for myself. I'm perfectly capable of keeping in my head the fact that I will have to make some time approximately three weeks from now to attend the scan. It's not something I'm likely to forget. Just because I'm not doing it your way doesn't mean I'm doing something wrong.'

She concentrated hard on the page; going over and over one word with her pen until he feared the paper would dissolve. But she didn't argue with him. The best he could hope for, for now, he supposed.

'Okay, so that's the appointments sorted for now. What next?'

'I want to have the baby in London.'

'Makes sense, considering you live there.'

'So you'll have to make arrangements to be up there, if you want to be around when it happens.' He nodded, able to see the logic in that. He waited, wondering whether she'd want him to make some more definite plans, but she seemed happy—or at least reluctantly willing—to leave it at that for now. Though he did notice the way her pen ripped through the paper slightly as she wrote the next word.

'Fine.'

'Seems to me like we can't really decide anything to do with dates until you've seen a doctor, though,' Leo said. 'So how about we leave that for now and move on to another part of the plan? What else is on your list that needs deciding now?'

When she didn't reply, he looked up from where his eyes had been following her pen scoring into the paper, to find her sitting with her mouth open and a hesitant look on her face. 'What?'

'You're right. We don't need to decide every-thing now.' She started to close the notebook, but Leo reached out and laid a hand across the page, trying not to notice the way that his skin tingled when it accidentally brushed against hers.

'Something's worrying you. Why don't you tell me what it is?' He tried to catch her eye, but she seemed determined not to meet his gaze. An alarm bell, deep in his belly, started ringing. 'What's the problem?'

'It's not a problem. It's just—' she took a deep breath and spat the words out '—I had all this worked out with scenarios, and different options and choices, and now that I'm sitting here at your kitchen table it feels weird.'

'What? Now that I'm a real person and not just an item in your schedule? Now that I get a say?'

She nodded. 'I am sorry. For turning up with it all finished and ready to present to you. I didn't mean to cut you out, to tell you this is the way it has to be. I just had to see for myself how I was going to make this work. And the only way to do that was to work it all out and write it down. I can see how it must have looked, as if I was dictating the whole of the rest of your life to you. But I didn't mean it that way.'

Her honesty eased that little knot of tension from his stomach, and he couldn't tell her how grateful he was for this acknowledgement that maybe she didn't have it all worked out after all. Funnily, her apology for creating the schedule in the first place made him want to help her with a replacement more than ever; he wanted to do whatever it took to make this work for them, even if it felt like seeing Exit signs being ripped down in front of him. Because what was an escape to him now? Sure, he could run. He could get far away from Rachel, throw money at the situation to keep the lawyers happy and have nothing to do with this woman and her child ever again. But he wouldn't. He couldn't.

And just like that his relaxed feeling was gone. He sat a little straighter in his chair, the tension in his neck and shoulders not allowing him to lounge. There was no escape now. Nothing for it but to plough on, into whatever it was his life held for him. He couldn't escape the facts: he was going to be a father. This woman, her plans and her notebooks, would be in his life for ever.

But not every part of his life. Rachel's presence had become an accepted fact between that Italian lunch and her turning up here. But just because he had her in his life, didn't mean he couldn't keep parts of it for himself. Keep part of himself safe. So she would be the mother of his child. He couldn't change that. But that was all she would be. He would stop these daydreams and night-time fantasies about that night. Forget the feel and taste of her lips and skin. He wouldn't fall into a relationship with her just because she was carrying his child.

'Let's just get this over with,' he said, forcing out the words. 'We have to talk about it some time, and we're both here now. What else did you have written down before?'

'Well…there was one part of the plan I had trouble with,' she admitted. 'Without knowing your financial position it was difficult to be accurate, so I came up with a number of different scenarios.'

'You should know, I'm not as well off as you might think.' He wasn't sure why he just threw the words out like that. Best defence perhaps, hoping to scare her off. Instead, he could see from her scowl that he'd offended her. He cursed under his breath. How could they misstep at *every* turn?

'And how would you know what I think about your financial position?'

'Well, we met at a fundraiser where the tickets cost two hundred quid a plate. It would be reasonable on your part to assume that I was loaded. I'm not,' he added, watching her carefully to see her reaction. She didn't even look surprised, never mind disappointed.

'If you remember, I thought you were crashing. So the price of the ticket is neither here nor there.'

She was impossible to second-guess this morning, Leo realised. But nothing he'd seen so far screamed gold-digger. He was cautious of money, and those who wanted it. And he had every reason to be. He'd grown up surrounded by it, rich and miserable. When he'd turned twenty-one, and for the first time could decide for himself how much of the family money he wanted to use, he'd decided the answer was 'none of it'.

He'd been selling his artwork since school, and when he'd left had set up a website and taken a few commissions, still trying to decide what he wanted to do with his life. When the paperwork had come through authorising his access to his trust fund, he'd decided once and for all that he didn't want a penny of it for himself. So he'd set up donations to charities, funded a few local projects he was interested in, and left the remainder in the bank, waiting until he could decide the best place to send it.

He'd saved almost every penny he'd earned, and as the commissions for his work increased, so did the nest egg he was building up. He'd wanted to buy a home, somewhere completely his, where he could feel safe. All he could afford was this wreck, a shell of a place when they'd exchanged the contracts, but it was his, and he loved it. He worked the renovations around his commissions, and the time that he spent in his studio, so progress had been slow, but he had relished every minute of the work.

His art had gained a reputation now, and it had been a long time since he'd had to worry where that month's mortgage payment would come from. And he could certainly support a child.

But he wouldn't see his son or daughter grow up with the sense of entitlement—to money, to people, to anything they wanted—that he'd seen from the boys at school.

'I'm not loaded, and I can't give you a specific figure right now,' he said eventually. 'I pretty much just turn everything over to my accountant and let him worry about it. But I'll do my bit, I can promise you that.'

Rachel reached down and pulled off her flip-flops; she threaded her fingers through the straps as she walked along the beach, swinging her arms and enjoying the feel of the sand between her toes. Well, Leo didn't seem to be in any hurry for her to see whatever he wanted to show her, she thought, as they ambled down across the sand. The tide was out, and the beach stretched before her, flat and vast. A dark stripe of seaweed bisected the view, and as they grew closer she detected its smell—raw, salty, and not entirely pleasant. She couldn't help but notice that Leo seemed to be getting more interested the closer they got. His eyes scanned the beach.

'Looking for something?'

'For *any*thing,' he corrected, though Rachel wasn't any the wiser for this clarification.

'Looking for anything.' She spoke seriously and nodded as if this made perfect sense to her.

'Come on, I'll show you.'

Leo grabbed her hand and towed her the last few yards across the sand, dragging her, as far as she could tell, to the largest pile of stinking seaweed.

'Ah, now I understand,' she lied, looking down and laughing, still completely clueless about what they were doing here. She could hardly be expected to play detective when her hand was trapped in his. When her every nerve ending and neuron seemed intent on those few square inches of skin where their bodies were joined. 'You love the seaweed. You think a city girl like me will be impressed by its… pungency?'

He laughed. 'Exactly. I brought you all the way down to the coast to enjoy the finest seaweed this country has to offer. No, don't be daft.' He threw her another smile, and gestured to the stinking pile with their joined hands. 'Let's get stuck in.' Abruptly, he dropped her hand and to his knees, before picking up a huge handful of the slimy green fronds and throwing it to one side.

She let out a bark of laughter, unable to hide her amusement at this grown man's pleasure at rooting through rubbish. 'And what exactly are we looking for?' She crossed her legs and dropped beside him, gingerly picking through the nearest weeds.

'Whatever the sea has sent us.'

She sat with the idea for a moment, trying to see if she could leave that statement as it was. If she could accept it. Nope.

'You're sure you're not looking for something in particular.'

'I'm sure. I've found all sorts down here. You never know what will turn up.' He looked up and his gaze met hers. When he saw that she still didn't understand, he rocked back on his heels. 'If it helps you to have a bit more of a plan, look out for driftwood. Something big, rubbed smooth by the sea.'

She frowned a little. His answer had taken her by surprise, and she didn't like the feeling. 'What do you want it for?'

'To make something beautiful. Something

for the house, or something to sell. I've found all sorts out here,' he went on—he must have seen she wasn't yet convinced. 'Jewellery, pottery, beautiful rocks and shells. Just have a dig around.'

Sitting on the sand, she couldn't do more than pick through the pile directly in front of her, so she clambered up onto her knees, getting used to the feel of the weeds slipping through her fingers. She snuck a glance at Leo from the corner of her eye, still trying to see where this exercise was leading. As if there was some part of him that was a complete mystery to her. He was wandering along the line of debris, kicking it with his toes at times. Unable to see anything but weeds and the odd carrier bag, she decided to catch him up.

'Any luck?' he asked as she reached him.

'Not—' She started to speak but then a glint of something on the sand caught her eye. She dropped to a squat on her heels like a toddler and carefully pulled the glass out from under the detritus. As she cleaned it off, an antique bottle emerged in her hand. She stared at it, taken aback by the appearance of this beautiful object. Leo came to stand behind her and peered at the bottle over her shoulder.

'Very nice.' He reached out to take it. 'May I?'

She handed it over and he turned it in his

hands, brushing off a little more sand and scrutinising the lettering.

'It's been in the water a long time, I think,' she said, just making out the figures '1909' on one side. She took it back from Leo and tested its weight in her hands. 'No message, though.' She peered into the neck, wondering if it had once carried a slip of paper.

Energised by her find, hitting gold her first time beachcombing, she started walking again, stopping often to pull aside some stone or vegetation, offering up shells and rocks for Leo's admiration.

Before long, she had pockets full of pretty shells, and her bottle tucked safely under her arm. She could feel the waves and the sand working their magic on her and Leo, as an easy chemistry and camaraderie grew between them. 'Do you find a lot of stuff out here?'

'Enough to keep me in hot meals and building materials.' She raised an eyebrow in question, too relaxed to be frustrated by his cryptic answer. But then she'd been so...abrasive, that first time they'd met, she couldn't blame him for being reticent about telling her about his life.

'You know, you never really explained what you do. I know I wasn't helping, being snippy about a trust fund and everything. I realise I got it wrong, then.'

He halted suddenly, evidently taken by surprise. When he started walking, there was something a little stiffer about his stride. 'Not entirely wrong.'

'But you said—'

'I said I'm not loaded. What I didn't tell you is that it's out of choice.'

Her brows drew together in confusion, and she glanced at Leo, encouraging him to continue.

He sighed before starting to speak again. 'My family has plenty of money. Pots of it, in fact. Too much. And I do have a trust fund.' Not something that would normally cause such distress, she thought. 'But I haven't spent a penny of it for years.'

'Why not?' It was none of her business, but she could tell this was something big, for Leo. Perhaps the tip of an emotional iceberg, something he didn't often talk about. And she wanted to know him.

'It's hard to explain. I want you to understand. I want you to know why I find it hard for you to pull out that plan… I'm not making life hard for the sake of it. It's all connected.'

Her heart ached at the note of vulnerability in his voice, the pain that he was clearly hid-

ing. And it soared a little, too, at the fact that
he was sharing this with her. Opening up to
her. But Leo's shoulders had fallen forward,
and a haunted look had crept over his face. She
reached for his hand, refusing to acknowledge
what that contact might signify, but needing
him to know that she was there to support him.
'I want to understand, Leo. Tell me anything
you want.'

'The money,' Leo said. It seemed as good a
place as any to start. He led them both away
from the water, to the very edge of the beach,
with the cliff creating a natural shelter around
them. He sat on the warm sand, and pulled
gently on Rachel's hand until she was sitting
beside him. 'I grew up with people who had
it—lots of it. Far too much. It didn't make
them happy, and it didn't make them good.
And there were people who thought I needed
it, desperately…' He paused but she didn't say
anything, just waited for him to continue. 'I
went to a very good school—and it was hell.'
    He gripped her hand, and she squeezed it
back. The warmth and comfort of her touch
flowed from her skin to his—he couldn't have
let go of her at that moment if he'd had to. He
wanted to pull her close, to bury his face in her
hair and his body in hers. Forget everything

about his past; ignore everything about their future. He wanted her lips on his, wanted to hear her chuckle with pleasure and sigh with satisfaction.

But he also wanted her to understand him. Wanted her to see why any hint of feeling trapped scared him so much. He needed her to know why he would never allow himself to be trapped in a relationship he couldn't get out of. And he knew he had to tell her everything.

'For some reason the other boys saw me as an easy—and early—target. To start with it was whispers about money. People accusing me of stealing from the other boys. Suggesting that money had gone missing from pockets and dorms. I tried to ignore it, thinking it would pass. And then they started talking about my mum. Insinuating that my "greed" ran in the family, that she was a shameless gold-digger who'd ensnared my dad for his money.

'She's from a different background from my dad, her family wasn't well off and his is loaded, and she married him when he was a widow with a three-year-old. That seemed to be all the evidence the boys needed.

'I couldn't ignore these whispers. I started to fight back, to defend my mum and myself, and it escalated. The older boys were determined to show me that answering back would get me nowhere. It turned violent, and nasty. I hadn't told anyone what was going on, but after a beating that left me bruised and heaving, I knew that I had to do something. My older brother—half-brother—was at school with me.'

'Did he help?'

Leo steeled himself to answer, but found his throat was thick, and his eyes stung. Even after all this time, he still couldn't think about what had happened without being close to tears.

'I'm not sure I understand,' Rachel said gently. 'I'm sure it must have been terrible, but it was a long time ago. You left that place—'

'Yes, and I will never go back.'

'Of course not, Leo. You're a grown man. No one can make you go back to school.'

He snatched his hand back, frustrated that after explaining the parts of his past that still caused the occasional nightmare, she could brush it off with 'you don't have to go back to school'.

'But I had to go back *then*.' The words burst out of him, just short of a roar. He'd had to go back time after time, year after year. Stuck in that place every day with the boys who hated him. Who thought up new and different ways to torture him.

'Couldn't you have left?'

'You think I didn't want that? Even when I

eventually told my father what was going on he didn't take it seriously. The bullies closed ranks when my parents spoke to the school. Told the headmaster that the bruises were from rugby. Or that *I'd* started a fight. They were so convincing. All the teachers fell for it. Sometimes even I found myself wondering if I was imagining it all. If I was going mad.

'I was trapped. Every morning I'd wake up in that dorm, and knew how my torture would pan out for the day. Taunts in the bathroom during break. Starving at lunch, too scared to risk the dinner hall. A few kicks in the changing rooms after games, somewhere it wouldn't show when I was dressed. And at night, I was locked in with them.

'The days the school knew where I would be and when, they would know, too. And ever since—I've needed a way out. The thought of being trapped—' He stopped abruptly. 'It terrifies me, Rachel.'

'You think I trapped you?' Her voice was flat and sad, more disappointed than angry.

'It doesn't matter, does it? Whether you did or not, it doesn't change the fact that—'

'That you want to escape and you can't.'

He rubbed his head in his hands, fighting against the fear to find the logic in his argument. 'I don't even know if I want to escape. What I would want if I wasn't…'

'Stuck.'

He nodded. 'You probably think I'm a complete jerk for telling you all this.' He felt like one. For admitting all the reasons he was terrified of what their lives were going to become.

She shook her head, though her expression was grim. 'I don't. I'm glad you told me how you feel. You can't help thinking the way that you do. I just wish it were…different.'

He reached past her to pluck a small piece of driftwood from the sand. The light played on it as he turned it over, and he kept his eyes focused on that, rather than meeting Rachel's gaze.

'How did you cope—at school?'

He looked across at her now, surprised she wanted to know more after what he'd just told her.

'I spent a lot of time at the beach.'

'Surfing? Swimming?'

'Some of the time. I was lucky in a way— the school was only a couple of miles from the coast, so I was able to spend a lot of time there. When I had to be on campus, I escaped to the art studio.' She looked at him in surprise. For some reason, he enjoyed that, throwing off her preconceptions of him. He was even able to crack a smile at her gaping expression.

'The art studio?'

'Yes—I'm an artist, didn't I mention that?'

'An artist.' She said the word as if it were something alien, obviously not believing him. He nodded, still playing with the driftwood as he took in her dropped jaw, her hands indignantly planted in the sand either side of her. 'You're an *artist*.'

A laugh escaped him, surprising him as much as her. 'I'm sure I mentioned it before.'

'And I'm certain that you didn't. What sort of artist?' She still hadn't wiped the incredulity from her face and he wasn't sure whether to be amused or annoyed that she found the idea of his occupation, vocation—whatever you wanted to call it—so laughable.

'A successful one, thankfully. That's what I wanted to show you this afternoon—my studio's down here rather than up on the cliff.'

'Right.' She drew the syllable out, as she examined his face, looking for hints of his artistic temperament perhaps. 'And the beachcombing, where does that fit into this?'

He breathed a sigh of relief that they were back on safer conversational ground. That she'd listened to his painful story, offered support, but moved on when he needed to. And his work he could talk about for hours. 'It's one of my favourite ways to find inspiration for my work and materials for the house. I've incorporated a lot of driftwood in the build. It's an ecologically sound way of working.'

'But doesn't it leave you at the mercy of the tides, or the water gods, or whatever force it is that throws up driftwood onto beaches? Wouldn't it just be easy to order the whole lot at once? I'm sure that there are suppliers with good green credentials.'

'I could do, I suppose, but I'm happy just taking opportunities as they arise. You never know what you're going to find. Like the floorboards for the living room. They just turned up in a reclamation yard. I could have bought brand-new timber last week and would have missed out on all that gorgeous character.'

'Yes, but you would have had a floor for a week by now.'

He threw her a grin and nudged her with his shoulder. 'What is it, princess? Upset that the place wasn't perfect for you?'

'Oh, don't give me "princess". I just think that while your way of doing things sounds lovely, in theory, when you have no real responsibilities, sometimes practical matters have to take a higher priority. Like a roof that doesn't leak. And a floor beyond the front door.' Not in the mood to joke about the house, then, he surmised.

'Well, then, I count myself lucky that you don't get a say in how I renovate my house.'

He stared her down, daring her to argue with him, so that he could remind her again that he would not be tied down by her. She might be carrying his baby, but that didn't mean that she could come down here and start telling him how to live his life, any more than he would dream of going up to London and telling her how to live hers.

She didn't take the bait. Instead she stood and started brushing sand from her jeans, and then walked back to the cliff path. He watched her for a few moments; then jogged to catch her up.

'Wait, I'm sorry. That wasn't fair of me. If you still want to, I'd like to show you the studio.'

She paused and glanced up at the house. Then looked back at him and softened. 'I'd like to see it. I can't believe I didn't know you're an artist. You didn't finish telling me how that happened.'

He started down the twisting path that led along the bottom of the cliff to his studio and workshop, wondering whether he could talk about his introduction to the world of art without reliving more of the pain he'd suffered at that time. He'd try, for her, for them.

'I told you I used to hide out in the art studio… None of the other boys seemed too keen to follow me there. Perhaps something to do with the belligerent old teacher who rarely left the room, Mr Henderson. I found it peaceful—it had these huge windows that let in the light, and you could see the sea in the distance. I'd spend lunchtimes hiding out in there and playing around with whatever materials the professor had in that week. One week, when I arrived, this huge hunk of driftwood was sitting on one of the tables. When I walked in the room, Mr Henderson looked at me, then at the wood, and then walked into the store room and left me there with it. Does that sound weird?'

She raised her eyebrow slightly. He'd take that as a yes.

'Okay, so it sounds kind of weird. I'll warn you, it might get weirder. I just wanted to touch the wood. It was as if I could see, no, *feel*, something beneath the surface. So I got some tools and started carving. It was as if the wood came to life under my fingers, and I found something beneath the surface that no one else could see until I revealed it.'

'You're right. Weird.'

He laughed.

'In a good way,' Rachel clarified, bumping Leo with her hip as they walked along. 'Weird, but cool. And there's a market for this? Secrets lurking in driftwood.'

'I know, it surprised me, too.' Leo smiled, thrilling at the energy Rachel's smile and teasing could create in him. 'But there is. A bigger one than I'd imagined, actually. Enough for me to put down a deposit on a shell of a house and to keep me in tarpaulin until I stumble upon some roof tiles. Anyway, we're here,' he declared as they rounded a corner and the studio came into view.

She ran a hand along the workbench, and enjoyed the sensation of the wood—warm, dry and gritty on the soft pads of her fingers. It was like meeting Leo afresh, seeing this room, and for the first time she was aware of how much she'd underestimated him. One glance at his beach-ready hair and surfers' tan and she'd written him off as a beach-bum trust-fund kid.

But this room showed her how wrong she'd been. It wasn't just the evidence of how much work had gone into the place—hours to fit out the studio: floor-to-ceiling window panels, cupboards and work surfaces. It was the art itself, each piece like a little peephole into Leo's character. Almost every surface carried pieces in various states of completion. The centre of the room was dominated by an enormous piece of wood. It must have been three feet across, and was nearly as tall as she was. And it seemed to be moving. It wasn't, she saw as she moved closer. It was just light playing over the wave-like carvings that made it seem that way. Constantly changing; constantly keeping her guessing. As she took another step closer she realised that it wasn't just one piece of wood, it was many, woven and flowing together. She wanted to glance across at Leo, to tell him she thought it was beautiful—more than that, it was astonishing—but she couldn't drag her eyes away. At last she reached out, wanting to feel the waves and light beneath her fingers, but Leo gently grabbed her wrist and stopped her.

'I'm sorry. I shouldn't have just—'

'Normally I'd say touch away. But I treated the wood this morning. So, what do you think?'

She finally managed to pull her eyes away from the piece and flicked her gaze up to his face. He looked a little anxious, she realised, as he waited for her verdict on his work.

'Leo, it's beautiful. I had no idea.'

'Ah, well, you know, I only come down here when the waves are rubbish.'

He was still standing close, his fingers still wrapped around her palm, and she pushed him lightly with her other hand. 'If I remember rightly, you told me you "sort of" had a job. I'm sorry, but this isn't sort of anything. You *are* an artist.'

He nodded. 'Like I said back on the beach. This is worth the scavenging, then?'

She nodded, her gaze fixed back on the waves, trying to see what it was that made the solid wood seem to shift before her eyes. Leo finally nudged her with his hip—'Earth to Rachel. I'm glad you like it. Really, I am.'

Suddenly she was aware how close he'd stepped to stop her touching the sculpture. How his hand still gripped hers, although it must be minutes—longer—since she'd dropped it away from the driftwood.

Though she'd felt hypnotised by the piece, it slowly filtered through to her that it and Leo couldn't be separated. The beauty of his work was part of who he was. And something about that made her feel as if she didn't know him at all. Didn't understand him. As if she no longer understood the situation they found themselves in.

She turned her face up to his, and tried to see the Leo she thought she knew in the features of this talented, passionate artist. She thought back to how quickly she'd written him off as spoiled and undisciplined when he'd told her he "sort of" had a job, and could have kicked herself for that lazy assumption. If she'd taken the time and care to actually ask him more about himself, she wouldn't be so blindsided now.

She'd turned her body when she looked up at him, and could almost feel the attraction pulling them together. He seemed taller—much taller—when she was in her flats, and from here she had a perfect view of his broad chest and shoulders, courtesy, no doubt, of hours in the water. Leo seemed to be studying her as closely as she was him, though she wasn't sure why. He wasn't the one who'd just had his entire perception of their circumstances change—again. But the intensity of his gaze was intoxicating, and she found that once her eyes met his she couldn't look away.

'I'm sorry—' Rachel hoped that speaking out loud might break the dangerous connection. Help her to re-establish some sort of calm. But Leo laid a gentle finger on her lips.

'You don't need to apologise.' The finger was replaced by a thumb, which rubbed across her lower lip, bringing sensation and longing with it. She felt her flesh swelling beneath his touch, ready for his kiss, begging for it. And Leo was reading the message loud and clear.

He dipped his head, and Rachel let out a little sigh, remembering all too clearly exactly what one of Leo's kisses promised. As she breathed in, and got two lungfuls of his salty, sea-tanged scent, she was tempted—God, so tempted—to forget the last point she'd made in her plan. The one she'd set in red, bold and underlined: *NO SEX*.

Leo's lips brushed against hers and she turned her head, so his kiss grazed across the corner of her lips and her cheek. She stifled a groan, half kicking herself for writing that into the plan, and half impressed with herself for making a decision when she was thinking more clearly than she was right now. Because she strongly suspected if she hadn't had a plan to follow in that moment, she would have been in serious danger of repeating past mistakes.

She took a deliberate step away from him, still not quite able to trust her commitment to her plan. Leo raised an eyebrow in question when she finally lifted her face to meet his gaze.

'I'm sorry. I should have been clearer before now.' Rachel took another step away and leant back against one of Leo's workbenches to steady herself. 'I enjoy your company, and I'm glad we're getting to know one another. I hope that we can be friends. But that's all that's on the table—friendship.'

Leo's hands dug into his pockets and he watched her from under heavy brows. 'You enjoy my company?' She could sense embarrassment washing over her features at the slow, deliberate way he spoke the words, conjuring memories of every pleasurable moment of their first and only night together.

His voice was low and gravelly as he spoke again. 'I would have thought a decision as important as that would have been in your plan.'

She opened her mouth to tell him that if he'd made it to the last page, he would have seen, would have known that it was. But he obviously read her expression too well and finally lost his serious look, bursting into an unexpected laugh.

'You did! You wrote "no sex" into the plan. You astound me, Rachel, honestly.' Except he looked more amused than astounded, what with the laughing and everything.

'It's important to know where we stand,' she told him, a little offended, if she was honest, that he could laugh so soon after their aborted kiss.

'Well, consider me well informed.'

Shouldn't he be a bit more…disappointed? Rachel thought as Leo walked over to the other side of the studio and started sorting through a stack of driftwood and bric-a-brac in one corner. It didn't make sense, the hollow, sinking feeling in her belly. Because a purely platonic relationship was exactly what she'd wanted. But Leo's easy acceptance of her rejection was as good as a rejection in itself.

'Here they are. I knew there were a couple in here.' From the pile he pulled two glass bottles, similar to the one she'd just plucked from the beach. 'They look nice together, don't you think? Perhaps for the windowsill in your room?'

He lined them up on the bench, but she was more interested in why he'd been so keen to walk away from that kiss. He was the one who'd started it, wasn't he?

'So you're happy to just be friends. You're not interested in anything more.' She tried to keep the words casual. To show only the friendly interest her head told her was reasonable, and not the roiling discomfort her heart demanded. 'Because I think if there's anything we need to talk about, we should do it now.'

The smile actually dropped from his face, and he looked a little worried, she realised.

'"More" is an interesting concept.'

Interesting? Of all the words she would use to describe what happened when they went for 'more', *interesting* would not be high on her list.

'If "more" is another night like that one back at your place, then I'm all for "more". As much "more" as is on offer.'

She actually felt her cheeks warm again— she'd not blushed like this since she was a girl.

'But I suspect that for you, "more" is something, well…more than that. If we can't do one without the other, then you're right. Friends is best.'

And again with the sinking disappointment. So he wouldn't mind more sex, but he didn't want a relationship with her. Well, then, they were in perfect agreement.

'Back to the house?' she asked, faking a jollity she didn't feel. 'My train's in an hour, so I probably need to make a move.'

'Of course. Don't forget your bottles.' She scooped up the antique glass and with a last look at the sculpture in the centre of room, she swept out.

'What's the hurry?' Leo jogged up the path behind her, lagging behind because he'd had to lock up the studio.

'Oh, I didn't realise I was.' A lie, of course. Because much as she knew that she couldn't allow herself to want a relationship with Leo, as much as the thought of being involved with someone who was happy to live with no roof till the right tiles came along filled her with dread, she still wanted a little time and space to lick her wounds. Just because she'd decided not to want him didn't mean she didn't want him to want her—however ridiculous that might be.

As they turned the corner and the house came into view, the sight of it made her feel better and worse at the same time.

'So the roof,' she said, as Leo overtook her along the path and held out a hand to help her over a small crop of rocks. 'Is there a...?'

'A plan?'

'Yes.'

'No.'

Not exactly what she wanted to hear. No, she didn't technically get a say in how he wanted to renovate his home. But if she were to come back here—and they were having a baby, how could she not?—it would be nice if the place was watertight. And there would be a baby before next summer. She was reassessing the way she made decisions, the way she relied on her plans, but was it unreasonable to expect that there might be a roof to sleep under?

'Don't worry, Rachel. The roof should be done any time now. I can absolutely promise it'll be finished by the next time you visit. The floor, too.'

She laughed, though still wasn't convinced. 'Sounds like luxury. So…I'll see you in London in a couple of weeks, for the scan? Do you want me to book you a hotel? I don't have a guest room. But you're welcome to my couch.'

'Don't worry; I'll sort somewhere to stay.'

'Are you sure? Because I—'

'I don't need you to organise anything. Relax. I'll take care of it. Do you want a lift to the station?'

'Oh, no need. I've already arranged a cab.'

He gave her a smile she wasn't sure how to interpret. 'Of course you have.'

CHAPTER EIGHT

'SO THIS "NO-SEX" THING. Remind me again, what kind of a rule are we talking about—a law, guideline or EU directive?'

Rachel shot Laura a look over her decaf Americano. It still took her by surprise sometimes that her slight, quiet, almost mousy best friend could cut to the chase quite so sharply. Laura had been thrilled for Rachel when she'd seen how happy she was about the baby, but too fascinated by far by her relationship with the father. 'Why are you bringing this up now? It's whichever one of those means that it's not happening. Ever.'

'I'm bringing this up because I'm about to meet him for the first time and you still fancy him.'

She took a couple of deep breaths, until she was sure she could speak impassively. 'He is quite attractive.'

Laura rolled her eyes. 'He got you home

from that party. I'm willing to put money on him being pretty special.'

Okay, so she was crazy to think she could pull the wool over her best friend's eyes. 'He's gorgeous, all right. I freely admit that he's gorgeous. But that wasn't why…' She trailed off, not wanting to incriminate herself by admitting to anything other than the most carnal feelings about Leo.

She glanced at her phone again, wondering what was taking him so long. All he had to do was show up. How hard could it be? So hard that the last time they'd had a scan appointment he'd called with a barrelful of excuses and then missed the first look at their baby.

With ten minutes to go before their previous appointment, she'd hit redial again and again. Voicemail. It had gone straight through to his messages ever since Leo had lost signal as he'd passed through a tunnel the last time he'd called. Two hours before. He couldn't have still been in that tunnel, so there was no reason for it not to have rung. She had tried to fight her anger down—it hadn't been Leo's fault that floods had closed all the train lines from the south-west. That the motorways had been clogged. That trees had been blown down and were blocking roads. But none of that changed the fact that she had needed him, and he hadn't been there. She needed a partner, her co-parent. She'd been excited for weeks about the scan, counting down the days until she would get a first glimpse of her baby. But in those past few hours since Leo had called with the news about the trains, all she'd been able to think about were her fears—what if the stick had lied to her, and she wasn't pregnant after all? What if they saw there was something wrong with the baby, if there wasn't a heartbeat? What if she had to face bad news without him?

She had hit redial again—and still there had been no response.

Checking the time as she'd hung up, she had taken a deep breath and squared her shoulders. She had to do this one on her own. Not that she'd had a choice; those last few hours had taught her something she should have faced long before then. She couldn't rely on Leo. It didn't matter how enthusiastic he was about the pregnancy, how good his intentions had been, she had to rely on herself, and no one else.

She'd gone into the ultrasound room alone and upset. The first glimpse of her baby should have filled her with complete joy, and it had; it was magical, emotional. But she hadn't been able to help but feel the loss of Leo by her side. When he'd finally arrived, Leo had promised her that he'd tried everything humanly possible to get there, but now, with less than five minutes to go until she was meant to meet him for their second scan, she was becoming nervous. What if he let her down again? What would she do if she couldn't trust him to be there when she—when they—needed him?

This time she'd asked Laura to come with her, to give her the support she knew she couldn't rely on Leo for.

'Oh, now, this is interesting.' Laura dragged her thoughts back to their conversation. 'This *is* new. If you didn't take him home because you were mad for his body, then this is something else entirely. I thought you told me that it was a moment of lust, not to be repeated.'

'It was!'

'No.' Rachel waited as Laura took a long sip of her coffee, and could practically see the words flying behind her eyes as she picked through them carefully, analysing, choosing an angle. 'You just said, or didn't say, that isn't true. So, what was it about him that caught your eye, other than his "quite attractive" looks? I know you, remember, and I know you don't make decisions like that at the drop of a hat.'

Rachel thought back to that night—the way Leo had teased her and made her laugh, made her relax. Fooled her into thinking that just for a night she could change her plan with no repercussions.

'He made me laugh; we were having a good time. I didn't expect—'

'For him to start baking in your oven.'

Rachel coughed as her coffee made a bid for escape through her nose.

'Thank you. Beautifully put.'

'Seriously, though.' Laura placed her coffee carefully on the table and held her gaze with a shrewd look. 'Are you sure that "just friends" is really the answer? You *like* him.' She held up a firm hand to stop Rachel's blustering protests. 'You can deny it all you want and I still won't believe you. And you have no reason to think that he doesn't like you, either. But you're not going to even explore what there is between you?'

'The baby—'

'Is the perfect excuse to give it a go, not run from it. So what is it that scares you about him?'

She stared into her drink for a long minute, trying to capture everything that Leo made her feel. The exhilaration of that night, the glimpse of a more relaxed life, the freedom when he made her laugh. The terror of everything she knew, understood and believed about her future suddenly being ripped away. 'Be honest with me. Do you think there's something…not right…about the way I like a plan, a schedule?'

Laura didn't drop her shrewd expression, though her eyes softened. 'Yes. Truthfully, I don't think it's healthy how anxious you are without one. And if you're starting to see that, too, perhaps now is a good time to be thinking about making changes. I hate to break this to you, darling, but there's no hiding from chaos now. You're going to have to find a way to—'

'No.' Rachel choked the word out of instinct, her gut revolting at the thought of that inevitability. And then felt instantly bad for snapping at her friend. 'Yes. I'm going to try. But the baby's enough chaos. Leo's just too much, and I can't trust him to be there when I need him.'

'You really are nervous.' Laura smiled, giving no hint that she was offended by her best friend snapping at her. 'It's cute. I don't think I've seen you nervous before.'

'I'm not nervous.'

'So the father of your child, the man you found literally irresistible five months ago, is going to show up in this coffee shop in ten minutes' time, and you're not even slightly nervous? Rubbish.'

Leo raced across the pavement, determined to get to Rachel before the second hand hit twelve, to prove to her that he could be the partner, and the parent, that she needed him to be. He'd barely seen her since the last scan. A couple of lunches in London, that was all, the last time just a coffee when he'd been in the city to meet with Will about the Julia House sculpture.

She claimed she hadn't been able to get a weekend off since that first time she'd been down in Dorset. But he knew the real reason, that she was still angry and upset that he'd missed that scan. And of course he could understand that. But he'd tried everything he could to get there on time. He'd hired a car when all the trains were cancelled. He'd waded through floodwater when the car had got caught in a soaked back lane and had conked out. He'd begged and bartered for lifts into the city, and when he'd finally made it, fourteen hours after leaving his house, he'd apologised until his voice was hoarse and she'd told him to stop. He just wanted to make things right, which, despite her assurances the last time he saw her, he knew they weren't.

He swung open the door to the coffee shop, and there she was. Her hair shiny and straight around her shoulders, a mug clasped in her hand, and, framed by her propped elbows, a neat little bump. His breath stopped at the sight of her. And then he saw that she wasn't alone, and his heart sank.

'Hi,' he said, as he walked up to the table, sending Rachel a questioning glance. He looked at the other woman and held out his hand. 'I'm Leo.'

She'd brought a friend to their ultrasound? There was only one reason he could think of that she would do that, and it made him cringe in regret. She couldn't trust him to be here. He'd let her down, and she wasn't ready to forgive.

'Leo, this is Laura.'

He watched the loaded look that passed between Rachel and her friend, and tried to translate it. *You want me to leave now he's here?*

He stood awkwardly as they gathered bags and finished coffees. The silence between him and Rachel stretched out onto the street, through goodbyes with Laura, down the corridors of the hospital, and into the waiting room. She maintained a clear foot of space between them, and every time he tried to close it, it pushed her further away. It was a relief when the sonographer appeared, breaking the tension in the hushed waiting room.

'Rachel Archer?'

He risked a small smile at her as they walked into the ultrasound room, and then didn't know where to look when Rachel pulled up her top and the technician tucked blue paper into her waistband. The sight of her skin gave him goose bumps, as he remembered how soft it had been under his lips and his body. Looking up at the ceiling, he took a deep breath, reminding himself that this really was not the right time to be thinking those thoughts. In fact, Rachel had made it more than clear in every strained silence since he'd let her down that there was no right time for those thoughts—and he had agreed with her, at least at first.

Because he shouldn't want anything more than friendship from her. He was already getting so much more than he had wanted. One night with this woman had already brought one lifelong commitment. A thought that still made him breathless—and not in a good way. It was crazy to embark on anything romantic, because what else could that bring other than more commitment? They could hardly date and see how it went. Because where did they go when one of them realised that it wasn't going to work out? Or what happened if she started thinking about a future and a ring, and he started to sweat? They should just concentrate on being the best parents that they could be, and try to be friends, as well.

But, God, she looked delicious. Her body curved in new places, her breasts were bigger, and her belly rounded. His child was growing in there, he thought, his mind boggling. He dragged his eyes away, though, realising suddenly that it probably wasn't brilliant form to ogle someone while they were in hospital, whatever the reason.

That thought sobered him. Because this scan wasn't just a chance to wave at the baby and hope that he or she waved back. He'd been reading up about what they should be expecting. And so he knew that the ultrasound was done for serious reasons, that it was for the medical professionals to check for health problems. That thought gripped him with a twist of anxiety and without thinking he reached for Rachel's hand. She flinched, though whether it was from him gripping her hand or from the gel being squeezed on her belly he couldn't be sure. But she squeezed his hand back and looked up to meet his eye. When she gave a little smile, he realised that she was as nervous as he was.

He watched the screen as the technician manipulated the ultrasound wand, and saw black and white shadows moving. He squinted, trying to make out what was what, but it wasn't until the technician pointed out the tiny head and limbs that he finally understood he was looking at his child. His son or daughter.

He'd spent so long thinking about all the ways his life had to change now, about the fact he'd woken up one morning and found himself painted into a corner, forced into fatherhood whether he wanted it or not, that he'd never stopped to consider that he and Rachel had done something so…so…miraculous. It was the only word he could grasp as he looked at the tiny life on the screen. A whole new life, created from nothing but the urgent, overwhelming desire of that night.

And seeing that miracle, and the one on Rachel's face as she saw it, too, the undisguised incredulity and rush of happiness, he couldn't help but be deliriously happy with her. Or help the tear that slid from the corner of his eye. It wasn't that he wasn't stomach-churningly terrified still, he just realised that that fear didn't have to be all-consuming. He could be worried to his bones about what effect this little child would have on his life, but still be absolutely, unbelievably happy that they'd made their baby.

He squeezed Rachel's hand a little harder, and she turned her face towards him, her eyes and cheeks lit with happiness and wet with tears.

As he watched, another tear snuck from the corner of his eye, and he smudged it away with his thumb.

'Everything looks good here,' the radiographer announced, breaking the silence and passing Rachel a tissue to clean off the gel.

The intimacy between them suddenly lost, Leo turned away, offering her some privacy.

They strolled from the hospital into the park opposite still dazed with happiness.

'Rachel, you know I'm sorry, don't you, that we didn't get to share this before? That I would have given anything to have been here.' He reached for her hand, needing the physical contact, desperate to know that they were back to being friends. That everything was right between them again.

To his surprise, she smiled, looking up at him, her eyes still a little damp. 'I know. I know that you tried, and I should have forgiven you a long time ago. I thought that I... that the baby...that we didn't mean enough to you. But I know that I was wrong.'

Didn't mean enough to him? He didn't know how it would be possible for anyone to mean more. Somehow his whole world had shrunk and expanded until Rachel was the shape of his whole future. He stopped walking, and held onto her hand a little tighter.

'Rachel, you have to know, you and the baby, you're everything. There are still days where I feel like I've got no idea how we got here, but I wouldn't change it for anything. Wouldn't wish for anything but what we have.'

His free hand brushed away another tear, just sneaking out from the corner of her lashes.

'I felt so alone—'

'And it kills me even thinking about it.'

'I know,' she said. 'I didn't say it to make you feel worse. It just made me realise how much I wanted you there. How much I wanted us to see our baby together. How much it means to me that we get to share this. It wasn't that I wanted *someone* there, Leo. I wanted you.'

He drew her close, swiping another tear as she hid her face in his chest.

'I feel the same,' he said into her hair. 'And it's frightening and exhilarating and it reminds me how much there is still to learn about this whole family thing. But we can do this, Rachel, and we can be brilliant at it. Be parents. Be more than that to each other.'

He dipped his head and pressed his lips to her mouth. It was quick and soft and sweet, and as he rested his forehead against hers he couldn't think of a moment in his life when he'd been more content than this. With his baby's heartbeat echoing in his ears, with Rachel's skin warm against his and the memory of her lips smiling against his fresh in his mind. All the reasons he'd fought this romance seemed to slip away. Every objection to keeping this woman at the centre of his life—the space she'd occupied since the moment they'd met—faded. The important thing, the only important thing, was that they faced their lives together. 'You're right,' she murmured, and he could hear her smile in her voice. 'We'll be brilliant.'

CHAPTER NINE

RACHEL EYED THE encroaching black clouds and glanced at the ETA on the taxi satnav. Four minutes. She crossed her fingers and hoped she could get inside before the storm broke. It was going to be a big one, and her jacket was buried in the bottom of her bag, stowed out of reach in the boot of the car. Either running up the pathway—she glanced at her patent pumps doubtfully—or digging through her bag, she'd be soaked in seconds.

The weather had been beautifully clear in London, and had only clouded over slightly on the train journey down. But once she'd climbed into the taxi from the station it had turned so dark it seemed like night. And the clouds just kept on gathering. It was almost impossible not to consider it an omen. Not that she had any reason to think this weekend would go badly. After the last scan she and Leo had spent a joyful afternoon together, laughing and joking, talking tentatively about the arrival of the baby, and generally being full of generosity and joy. There was no reason to think that today would be any different.

Except that when he'd called her at lunchtime—inviting her down to Dorset for the weekend—there had been something in his voice that worried her. Behind his words had been an edge of something nervy and taut. Why didn't she take the afternoon off, he'd said, and come straight down to the cottage? She'd bitten down on the word *no*, and thought about it for a second, glancing at her calendar. It would mean moving her Monday around, but there was really no reason she couldn't... It was the perfect chance to put her new life decisions in action and try something spontaneous for a change. To ignore her plan for just a few hours and see where the afternoon took her.

She'd cleared it with Will and treated herself to a cab straight to her flat and then the station, her belly fluttering with the excitement of her first spur-of-the-moment action in years.

But as the car turned the final corner and the cottage came into view, Rachel's stomach sank, and she felt the cool damp fingers of fear and disappointment trickling down her collar, as icy as the imminent rain. The pile of builders' material in front of the house had shrunk considerably, but Rachel's eye was drawn to the roof, where a bright blue tarpaulin stood out like a flag against the grey sky. The tile-less corner of the house was very small, but very bare nonetheless.

And just like that she felt the significance of that omen grow. He'd promised. She'd trusted him that the house would be more habitable now—that it would at least be watertight. She was here, trying to live a little freer, trying to make their family work, and he had let her down before she'd even stepped inside. A crack of thunder threw her eyes to the sky and she knew that she'd have to run to the door. She just had to hope that she would be drier inside than she would be out here, as the first marble-sized drops of rain reached her.

Leo, umbrella in hand, swung open the front door when she was halfway up the path. 'I'm so sorry,' he shouted as he ran towards her, umbrella aloft and reaching for her bag. Another peal of thunder tore across the sky. 'I only just saw the taxi—'

'I'm fine,' she said as they reached the front door and Leo stood back to let her through. She glanced around her at the living room as she wiped the water from her face and brushed down the front of her sweater. At least he'd lived up to his promise of a floor.

'You're not fine. You're angry,' Leo said, looking at her.

Of course she was angry. How could she be expected to trust a man who didn't think a house in a thunderstorm needed a roof? Who couldn't see that something like the small issue of your home being watertight might be important? Especially when he had a guest. Who was pregnant—with *his* child.

'What's up?'

She shouldn't bite. They needed to be civil to one another if they were going to make parenting together work. She would just have to learn. 'What's up? The house still doesn't have a roof!'

'Oh, that. Most of it's finished, but there was a slight problem with the calculations, and there weren't enough tiles. I've got some more on the way. You're really annoyed about the progress of the building?'

'I'm really annoyed that it might rain indoors tonight.'

'Don't worry about that. It's only a small patch, and your room's on the good side. The roof's lined with plenty of tarps. The ceilings are all totally dry. I can't see any water getting in.'

'That's not the point.' Her hair was dripping cold water down the back of her neck, and she shivered. She pulled it into a ponytail and bundled it up onto the top of her head, using the distraction to try and temper her anger. 'You said that it would be finished by now.' The words came out icily cool, and she prided herself on keeping her fury under wraps.

'So I'm running a little late. It'll be done soon. There were a couple of other jobs that I wanted to do first. Wait.' He stopped his pacing, which had taken him from her side and back to the window, checking on the progress of the storm. 'Why are you so annoyed?'

With his casual disregard, she finally lost it. 'In case you hadn't noticed, you're going to be a father in a few months. Which means—I hope, or I hoped—that you might want your child to visit. How can I bring a baby into a house that doesn't have a roof?'

He stared at her, his eyes wide and his body language heading towards guarded as he planted his hands on his hips. 'The baby isn't due for months. There's plenty of time before then. I promise it'll be done by the time—'

'Another promise! How am I meant to believe this one, when the last one meant nothing?' She pulled her sweater over her head as she was talking, scattering raindrops everywhere, and forcing icy water from her hair down her back. Her shirt underneath was damp, too, and she shivered.

'It'll get done when it needs doing! Can't you trust me to know when that is?'

She rolled her eyes in disbelief, and dropped her voice as the fight left her and disappointment set in. 'I'm standing in a roofless house in the middle of the storm. Of course I can't trust you.' She shivered again, water still dripping down the back of her neck, her skin turning chilly and rising with goose bumps. She just wanted to get warm, and dry. And away from Leo and his empty promises. She grabbed her bag, brushing off Leo's offers of help, and headed for the kitchen and the stairs. She stormed up to her room and then dropped on the bed. Rubbing the heels of her hands into her eyes, she forced down tears. Why hadn't she expected this? Why did her disappointment make her feel so utterly broken?

Pulling herself together, she dug in her bag for dry clothes, and headed to the bathroom. When she walked back into her room, wrapped in cosy cashmere and with her hair turbaned into a towel, it was to find Leo on his hands and knees on the floor.

'You looked cold.' He glanced over his shoulder as he spoke. 'I thought you might like a fire.'

Rachel dropped down on the bed and gave Leo a long look. Her eyes darted to the ceiling, looking for damp, or any other sign of the storm that was shaking the windows. It looked dry, as Leo had said, and the heavy, guilty feeling in her belly made her wonder whether she'd been slightly hasty with her temper.

Suddenly, the fire caught, and Leo sat back on his heels, his face fully caveman smug. As the flames licked from the kindling to the wood—which looked suspiciously like the floorboards downstairs—she dropped onto the floor between the bed and the fire, sneaking her bare toes towards the heat.

Leo sat next to her, and nudged her shoulder with his. 'I know I said it would be done by now. And it almost is. But I'm sorry I disappointed you.'

'And I'm sorry for snapping the minute I arrived.' She let her shoulder rest against him, his heat adding to that of the fire, making her feel drowsy.

'You know these things take time. The materials don't just appear when I click my fingers. I can't do this according to your plan.'

She sighed, seeing how far apart they still were on how their lives would unfold. 'I know I said I'm going to be more flexible, but some things have to be done to a plan. Some things aren't safe, or sensible, or reasonable without one.'

'And some things work better. Sometimes we're happier.'

'Sometimes *you're* happier.'

He nodded. 'You're right. I am. But we need to meet somewhere in the middle. We need to find a way to do things that keeps us both happy. So if you're prepared to accept my apology for the roof not being finished, then maybe we can take another look at that master plan of yours. See what else we need to work out.'

She agreed, feeling a bit dreamy by the fire with the warmth on her face, the carpet soft between her toes and the bedspread squidgy behind her back. Those first few months of feeling exhausted had faded, but now six months pregnant and still keeping her usual unsociable hours—in the office by seven in the morning, often still there late in the evening— afternoon naps had become a standing fixture of her weekends.

She didn't move when Leo reached out to pull the fire guard back across, or when he reached above her to pull back the bedspread, even though it was more than tempting to turn into his shoulder, soak up more of his warmth and his smell. She was cold again when he stood, leaving her on the floor, but then he reached for her hands, pulled her to her feet and then back towards the bed. 'You look like you need sleep more than you need an argument.'

She couldn't disagree with that, and tucked herself between the sheets, wondering, for a fleeting second, what would happen if she kept hold of his hand and pulled him in after her. Disaster surely, probably, but just for now it would be… Perhaps it was best that sleep was pulling her eyelids closed, taking the decision from her hands.

She woke to the sound of pans clashing in the kitchen, and glanced at the clock on the bedside table. She'd slept for more than an hour. She stretched out under the bedspread, savouring the warmth in her limbs and on the side of her face. The fire in the grate was still burning strong, and it was no easy thing to drag herself out of bed, and pad downstairs to a man she'd practically fallen asleep on mid-argument.

'Hi.'

As she reached the bottom of the stairs, Leo was standing across the kitchen, his back to her, stirring something on the hob. But what caught her eye was the spread of papers on the table. Coloured pencils were scattered across pages peppered with arrows, exclamation marks and doodles. When she looked closer, she recognised the headings from her own plan, each one in the centre of a sheet of paper. And a couple she'd saved to talk about later: names, visitation, nursery.

She remained standing, astonished that Leo had started to plan for this baby, and admiring the beauty of what he'd produced. Most of it was indecipherable to her. Scribbles and arrows and more question marks than answers, from what she could see. But the doodles were what held her attention. Though that wasn't really the right word for them. They were miniature works of art, tucked into corners, and they told her more than she'd ever thought she'd know about what was going on in the mind of the man who had drawn them. A baby's head cradled in a muscular arm, unmistakably Leo's. A shadowy sketch that looked remarkably similar to the picture of their ultrasound. A woman sitting on the edge of a bed, her naked back covered by a fall of shiny hair. Rachel blushed, recognising herself.

'Afternoon.' Leo turned to her, holding a couple of mugs.

'There's chicken and vegetables as well, but I wasn't sure what you were up to these days…'

'Chicken sounds great.' Her belly gave a roll

of thunder to back up her words. 'Thanks. This is brilliant.'

Leo set the plates down on the table, sweeping aside his papers. He subtly tucked away the one with the sketch of her, she noted, from the corner of her eye.

'You saw my plans, then.'

'I did. They're beautiful…'

They'd taken to talking a couple of times a week. At first she'd thought that it was to sort out practical stuff, but gradually this had turned instead into a brief catch-up, and then they had spent long, lazy evenings and Sunday afternoons discussing the latest fundraising for Julia House, what the tide had thrown up, how the guy at the rec yard had found the perfect tiles for the kitchen. Face to face, conversation flowed more easily still, as she relaxed into his company.

'It's mostly what we've already talked about. It just all fell into place, and I could look at it in a way that made sense to me.'

'You've made it beautiful.'

She soaked up the smile he gave her, as warm as the fire upstairs.

'Eat first, talk second?'

'Perfect,' she agreed, digging into her dinner.

Once their plates were cleared away, she couldn't help her eyes wandering to Leo's plans, keen to see what he'd come up with and how it would fit with what she'd written. Leo must have spotted her not so subtle perusal.

'All right, then, get your notebook out. I know you're dying to.'

Why bother to deny it? She nipped up to the bedroom and grabbed her plans, and was back at the table before Leo had the chance to brew another coffee.

She pulled out her A3 plan as Leo placed a cup of black coffee in front of her. She flicked her eyes up and parted her lips to ask a question. 'Decaf,' Leo said, pre-empting her. She held his gaze a moment longer, before letting her eyes drift back to her plans.

She shuffled their papers and tried to match up Leo's to her own. Most of the practical stuff was covered: the dates of her midwife appointments; which hospital she was planning for the birth; due date, maternity leave and annual leave. So when she looked down at her plan, all the easy questions were dealt with, which left them with the tricky one they'd been skirting around for months now: access and living arrangements.

Leo was entitled—and deserved—to see his son or daughter as much as possible; she had no intention of ever denying that. But that didn't make it easier. They lived hundreds of miles apart, and their careers kept them there. And that meant that their child would have two homes, and that as parents they would be constantly shuttling between the two. The idea of a newborn was terrifying enough. When you added a three-hour train journey into the mix, it was suddenly more terrifying still.

'I think we need to talk about what happens after the baby's born,' she started. 'I need to be in London for the birth, and I can't see that it would be good for the baby to move around a lot in the first few months. From the advice I've read for separated parents, the best thing for a new baby is a consistent routine when it comes to seeing the secondary par—'

'Secondary?' She sat back in shock at the sudden hint of anger in Leo's voice. 'I'm sorry, when—exactly—did I get demoted?' His shoulders were fixed into a straight, solid line, and his face was flushed with emotion.

And this was why they'd put it off for so long, she thought. It was a minefield. She tried to keep her own voice calm, to defuse the situation.

'You've not been demoted, Leo. Please don't think that's what I'm trying to do. But unless you've suddenly grown the apparatus to feed a child then I'll have to be the primary caregiver. It would be the same if we were a couple, if we were married. It's just a word.'

He glared at her, and she realised that it wasn't just a word. Not to him at least.

'You're pushing me out.' His shoulders were still up and his face tense, and she realised he had been building up to this. She'd sensed it occasionally on the phone, an edge of concern and suspicion whenever they skirted around the issues of access and contact. She reached for his hand, wanting to calm the situation, but the contact of his skin on hers made her anything but.

'Leo, trust me. We are going to find a way that we are *all* happy. All three of us.'

'And how exactly are we going to do that when you hold all the cards and get to call all the shots?' He almost hissed the words as he pulled his hand away from hers, and then sat back in his chair and crossed his arms.

'We make this plan together. Tell me what you want and we will find a way to make it work.'

'Fine.' He ground the words out through gritted teeth. 'I want to be there. I want half the time, half the responsibilities. Half the holidays and Christmases. And I want it legal and in writing.'

'I don't understand where this is coming

from.' Bewilderment kept her voice gentle, questioning. 'For months you've baulked at even the thought of a plan or a schedule. Now you're demanding it? What's changed?'

'What's changed is you demoting me to a secondary parent! What's changed is you pushing me out.'

'And you refusing to trust me.'

She rested her head in her hands and took a couple of long, calming breaths. Parents at loggerheads didn't help any child—they would have to find a way through this.

'Let's start from the beginning,' she suggested. 'I go into hospital and the baby is born. When do you want to visit?'

'Visit? I don't want to visit.'

So starting from the beginning was no help. Was there nothing that they were going to be able to agree on? Leo's anger had been so sudden and unexpected she had no idea how to handle it.

'I want to be there for the birth. I want to be a part of everything. I thought I'd made that clear.'

She viscerally recoiled at the thought of it, of him seeing her groaning and exposed. 'No way. I know we're going to share a lot, for the rest of our lives, in fact. But can't you grant me a little dignity?'

'You don't want me there.'

'You're putting me on the spot,' she countered, trying to keep up with his arguments. 'I never even considered you might *want* to be there. I'd already thought—'

'You've already planned. What a surprise. Tell me, then, what have you planned?'

'I'd like Laura to be there during the birth, and she's said that she'll do it.'

He shook his head as if she'd disappointed him, and he'd expected it all along.

'And where do I fit into any of this? Or am I meant to just miss out on the first few weeks?' His voice broke, betrayed the fear and despair she sensed behind his anger. If he'd just tell her what was wrong, why he was finding it so hard to trust her, maybe they'd have a way of working this out.

She placed a hand over his, trying to soothe. 'So let's agree on something we're both happy with.'

'I want to be at the birth.' For a few moments, all she could see, hear, smell was blood, guts and embarrassment. She swallowed down her automatic refusal.

'Head end only. If I change my mind on the day you respect my privacy. And I want Laura, too.'

He looked up in surprise. 'Okay, I can live

with that. But when we get home, it's just the three of us.'

She nearly choked on her coffee. 'Oh, no, you can't think that you're moving in with me.'

Hurt twisted his features again. 'How else am I meant to be a father? Of course I'll be there. I'll sleep on the couch, if that's what you're worrying about. I'm not assuming that we'll…'

She shook her head again. Already able to see the argument she was walking into, and starting to feel shame colour her cheeks. This was something she should have talked to him about. She shouldn't have assumed that she could decide this without him. But the damage was already done. She hadn't meant to hurt him, but he seemed to be blindsiding her at every turn, wanting things she'd never imagined he would.

'I'm sorry, Leo, but I don't think it will work. For a start, there's not enough room.'

'It's a pretty small couch, you're right. I'll buy one of those blow-up mattresses or something.'

'That's not what I meant. I mean there's no room because my mother's going to be on the couch.'

'Your mother?' The words whipped out of him, stinging Rachel with their sharp edges

of disappointment and distress. 'Let me get
this right. So far your friend's going to be at
the birth of our child, and there's no room for
me to care for our newborn baby after you
come home because you've invited your mum
to stay. And you still don't think you're pushing me out.'

The worst part was, he was right. She had
pushed him out. Regret swelled in her chest,
and tears threatened at the corners of her
lashes. She hadn't intended to do it, to plan
without even making room for him. 'I'm
sorry. I didn't think of it that way. I just…I
just needed a plan. And I knew I couldn't push
you. And my mum was offering help, insisting
really. I didn't know what to do, so I took it.'

'This isn't meant to be about making either
one of us happy, Rachel. Or your mother—or
Laura, for that matter. It's meant to be about
what's best for our child.'

'You really think you have to tell me that?
That I'm not thinking about what's best for
him every single minute? I can't believe you
would accuse me of that.'

'And you don't think that what he needs is
both his parents? Unless you can give me a
very good reason why my being there is bad
for our child, I'll be moving into your apart-
ment. If there's not room for your mother, too,

then she can book into a hotel. But my need to be with my child, and my child's need to be with his parent, trumps hers.'

She rubbed her face in her hands, knowing that he was right.

'I can see from your face that you agree with me.'

'I'm sorry. Of course you can stay. I'll speak to Mum.'

And with that concession, the fire fell out of both their arguments. Leo's shoulders softened, and he reached out a hand for hers. 'Thank you. I just don't want to miss anything. Not a minute.'

'I know, Leo. But I'm not the enemy. I don't know why you can't trust that I just want what's best for our child.'

'I do.'

'That's not what you were saying a minute ago, when you were talking solicitors and formal access.'

'Then don't make plans without me.' He grabbed a sheaf of his sketches and spread them out on the table. 'Here. Everything that was in your plan, as I remember it. Well, almost everything.'

She looked over the sheets and realised what he meant. There was nothing about 'no sex' here. She glanced up at him. Was it not here because he didn't want it to be? Or because they had both been so vehement about it before that he thought they didn't need it. She wasn't sure what she had to say about it anyway. She was still bristling a little from his accusations.

'So you've told your parents about the baby.'

She looked up at him, shocked by his question. 'Of course I've told them. He'll be here in a few months. I wasn't just going to turn up with him after he's born.' And then something occurred to her. 'Don't tell me you haven't told yours…'

He held up his palms in a sign of defeat. 'I haven't really known where to start.'

'How about, *Mum, Dad—I've got some brilliant news…*?'

He raised an eyebrow. 'Is that how the conversation went with your parents?'

'Actually, I used those exact words.' She'd chosen them carefully, hoping that they might pre-empt her parents' concern.

It had taken her a couple of weeks to build up the courage to call her parents, knowing how much they were going to worry over her, sensing how that worry was going to threaten her own peace of mind. But eventually she had picked up the phone.

Once her mother had regained the power of speech, a flood of concern had followed. Why hadn't they met this man? Were they in a relationship? Had someone taken advantage of her? Had she informed the police?

Rachel had moved the phone away from her ear, trying to let their worries fall between the phone line and her brain, not letting them in. It was only when they started talking about getting in the car and coming to support her through this 'traumatic time' that Rachel realised that she had to put a stop to this.

'Mum, Dad. Please listen. I didn't take unnecessary risks. I wasn't taken advantage of. I'm thrilled about this baby, and I'd like it if you could be pleased for me, too.'

Stony silence.

Eventually they'd given muted congratulations, but Rachel had known as she'd hung up the phone that they would let their concerns about how their first grandchild was conceived spoil their excitement.

But Rachel wouldn't. She'd told them that it was brilliant news, and she'd meant it. Because however she might feel about Leo, she was in no way confused about what she felt about their baby. She supposed it was too much to hope that her parents would see it the same way.

But at least she'd told them. And apparently Leo hadn't even bothered to do that.

'You've told them nothing?'

His body language closed up, his arms crossing over his chest as he pushed his chair back from the table. She wondered what it was about his family that made him so…defensive. Like an animal that had been hurt before and was determined to avoid it happening again. Did this all come back to his brother, and school? 'It's not like we talk a lot.'

'And you didn't think that the fact that you're expecting a baby is something worth phoning home about?'

'You don't understand, Rachel.'

'Then tell me.' She leaned forward, making it impossible to escape into the space he'd created for himself. Impossible for him to run from her. 'Explain what's going on, because I don't understand, and if I don't understand, then how can we make it better?'

'There's nothing to tell.' The arms folded tighter. 'It's not a big deal.'

'Of course it's a big deal.' She couldn't let this drop, couldn't see something causing him pain and walk away from it as if she didn't care. This man had been on her mind every day for the past six months. Every day since they'd met, her heart had grown a little closer to his, as their lives had entwined, until she wasn't sure where hers ended and his began.

And every day, she'd cared a little more, and her hurts and his were as tangled as their lives.

'We're having a baby in three months' time, and you haven't told your family about it. It makes me worry about you. That there's something wrong that I don't know about. Something hurting you. Is this something to do with what happened at school? Because your father wouldn't pull you out?'

He sighed, and when he spoke his voice shook a little. 'That's part of it. But I wasn't going to put it off for ever.'

The tremble in his voice nigh on broke her heart, seeing this big tough guy, moments ago demanding to be put through the trials of the birthing suite, cowed and afraid of talking to his family. 'But ignoring it isn't helping, either. When are you planning on telling them?'

'Tomorrow. It's Mum's birthday. She called this morning and told me she's having a family lunch tomorrow. Wouldn't take no for an answer. She asked me if there was anyone I'd like to bring and I thought that this might be as good a time as any…'

She snorted a gentle laugh at his naive plan, that they would just walk in there with her big belly and that would be that, while trying to fight down her panic at this sudden swerve to their weekend. But Leo's serious face and lines borne of worry and fear firmed her resolve. He needed her there with him. She couldn't let him down just because she was uncomfortable with surprises.

'This is your family, your problem, so we can do this your way. No plan required. I'm not going to tell you what you should do. But I think talking with them could be a good thing. The very fact that you don't want to makes me think that it's a bigger deal than you're letting on.'

'Sometimes you're too smart for your own good. You know that?'

He spoke with a smile, and she held his gaze for a moment longer than was strictly friendly. And then she couldn't look away. She could feel something building between them. Something warm and strong that started in her belly and reached out through her fingertips, jumping the distance he'd put between them and pulling her in. His fingertips stretched out on the tabletop and just brushed against hers. She held back a gasp at the prickle of awareness concentrated in the pads of her fingertips, and pushed them a little harder into the grain of the wood. Schooling them not to grab him. Because that was what every hormone-fuelled impulse in her body was screaming at her to do. To grab that hand, seize the heat simmering between them and bury the remnants of their harsh words and misunderstandings in a kiss. Or, preferably, more.

But when Leo reached a little further, and buried her palm in his, his touch wasn't sensual. His eyes shifted, and it was pain, not desire, in his features. Her own momentary desire morphed into compassion as she read his change in mood.

'It was my brother,' Leo said baldly, the words barely inflected. 'At the very centre of it all. The bullying. He started it, he encouraged it, and he's no less cruel now than when we were children. When Dad spoke to the school, Nicholas somehow convinced the teachers, and in turn my parents, that there was nothing wrong. That I was attention-seeking. In the end Dad thought it would be character-building for me to stay.'

It was disgusting, made her feel physically sick. She could never imagine being treated that way by her family, and her heart ached for Leo. She squeezed his hand back. 'Leo, I'm so sorry. I can't believe your father—'

'No, it wasn't him. He had no idea what was really going on. You don't understand. Nicholas is…well, he can be very charming. And very convincing. I really do think that my father thought he was doing what was best. And it wasn't until later that I discovered Nicholas was at the root of everything. By then I'd left school and left home and it didn't seem worth tearing the family apart by bringing it up. My mother is happy as things are. She loves my father and he adores her. As long as Nicholas and I can keep our distance, she stays happy.'

'And I'm guessing it's mostly you who keeps your distance. It doesn't sound like your brother would be so considerate. You must love your mum very much, to do that for her.'

'Of course I love her. She's my mother.'

'Do you think she's going to be excited to be a grandmother? Is it her first? Nicholas doesn't…'

'No. Thank God. And yes, she's going to be thrilled. That's why I thought…at her birthday…'

'Whatever you decide. Whatever you need. Let me know.'

He turned her hand over in his and pressed a kiss to her palm. She shivered as his lips brushed her skin, and cupped her fingers around his jaw, just brushing against the ends of his hair.

But seeing him so upset, it was impossible not to try and help him. Not to reach for him and offer comfort. It sounded better that way, she told herself. Convincing herself that this was a selfless act, purely to make him feel better, and not to satisfy the ache that had travelled between heart and belly for the past few months. Ever since the night she had first met Leo.

As she reached across the table to him she felt their baby shift inside her, and dropped her other hand to her belly, rubbing at the elbow, or heel, or whichever body part was giving her belly a corner.

She remembered the first time it had happened, as she had lain on the couch, laptop balanced on her almost flat belly. Just a little flutter, almost nothing, but *everything*. The first time she'd truly felt pregnant. She'd dropped her work and reached for the phone, thinking of nothing but sharing this moment with Leo. Wanting him to share the rush of adrenaline and emotion.

Now his eyes followed her hand, watching closely as her hand moved over her tummy.

'Can I...?'

The yearning in his face was as strong as she had ever seen it. But this time it wasn't her body he wanted. Well, not exactly.

'Do you want to feel?' She pushed her seat back from the table at the same time as he stood. But standing over her, he hesitated. So she gently took his hand and guided it to where she could feel the baby kicking.

Rachel tried to keep her feelings motherly as Leo gently rubbed her stomach, following the kicks and movements of the baby. But with him standing over her, reaching down, she was surrounded by his body. Everywhere she looked there was tanned forearm, broad chest. That salty smell that was so unmistakably him. And this was wildly inappropriate, she told herself. He'd only come over here, was only touching her, because she was carrying his child. As far as she knew, he saw her as nothing more than an incubator right now. It had certainly been weeks, months, since they had even spoken about the fact that they had once been so intimate with one another. She had no reason to think that he wanted anything other than friendship from her. So she should just pull these pregnancy hormones of hers in line and stop fantasising about the other parts of her body that hand could be touching right now.

Rachel looked towards the ceiling, still trying to find a safe place for her gaze to rest. But it collided with Leo's intense blue stare. His hand remained on her belly, but, somehow, the touch changed. No longer curious, it was suddenly sensual. Caressing rather than exploring. His other arm rested along the back of her chair, and he leaned on it a little further. Bringing his face fractionally closer to hers. Just enough to fill her entire field of vision with the clean lines of his face and the coarse chaos of his hair. And her nose with his scent. And every single nerve-ending with the memory of how he could make her body sing. She tipped her head and closed her eyes.

His lips brushed against hers. Soft, but not hesitant. Deliciously assured and practised. Familiar but new, teasing her with all he had learnt about her since the moment they'd met. As Leo's hand found her waist, or what was left of it these days, she parted her lips with a moan, and twisted in her chair, snaking her arms up around his neck and pulling his body closer. He wasn't the only one who wanted to touch.

Somehow all the reasons this had seemed like a bad idea faded to nothing in the face of this connection with their child. With the passion that she felt for him and the love that they shared for the life growing inside her. And the love she felt for him, she realised. The love that had been growing alongside their child as she'd learnt more and more about its father. An artist who saw beauty in everything, the sublime in the ordinary. A son who sacrificed his own happiness to protect his mother. A brother who endured rather than confronted to save tearing apart his family. And the man who had helped her face her fears, and realise that not everything that terrified her should be avoided. Not this. Especially not this.

But she *was* afraid. She was afraid that Leo didn't feel the same way. That their differences still amounted to more than what kept bringing them together. But not so afraid that she was going to run.

God, she tasted incredible. He nipped out his tongue, tasting and teasing, as he desperately tried to catch his brain up with his libido. But it wouldn't cooperate. It was so flooded with sensation and need that there was no room for anything rational.

His hands cupped beneath Rachel's elbows and he pulled her to her feet. She was stretching up on tiptoe to reach his mouth, and it arched her body into his, their child pressed firmly between them.

'God, I've wanted to do this for so long.' He ground out the words between kisses, capturing her every gasp and moan with his lips. 'This—more—everything.'

At the word 'more', she pulled back, concern clear on her face.

'More?' His mind was thrown back to that day she'd told him there could be no sex between them, because she could never be happy with something just physical. He'd been an idiot. He wanted her in every way, in every part of his life. As he'd sat and sketched out their plans, he'd come to see that they all revolved around her. She was at the centre of his every hope and desire for the future.

'Not just that kind of more,' he said, too far gone to sugar-coat, to look for pretty words. 'I want you, Rachel. In every way possible. More. More of everything.'

His ego thrilled at the smile on her lips as he led her upstairs.

CHAPTER TEN

HE STROKED A strand of her hair as it pooled on his chest, his eyelids heavy and his body sated. 'Morning,' he said with a yawn, glancing at the curtains and guessing the time. 'I could stay here all day.' He kissed her gently awake and pulled his arm tighter round her. 'But we have to go tell my mum she's going to be a grandma.' He wanted to share their news, their joy, with his parents. Wanted to make Rachel a part of his family. Being so close to her, after months of denying how he felt, didn't seem like enough. The only way forwards from here was to face the demons from his past so that the three of them could move on. Together.

Because he wasn't scared any more. He was walking into this relationship with his eyes open. He couldn't be trapped somewhere he'd gone voluntarily. They were in charge of this situation, and no one else. And they could take this relationship anywhere they wanted.

'You're right, you know. I should have told them ages ago. So let's go and do it together.'

She smiled at him, reached up and brushed a soft kiss on his lips. 'Let's do it.'

As the car advanced up the driveway, Rachel's eyes widened. Leo tried to imagine seeing the house for the first time. The driveway wound through the grounds to show off every beautiful angle of the building. It offered views of leaded windows, grand entrances, and a glimpse of formal gardens. The redbrick building sat proudly in the landscape, its turrets and chimneys reaching up towards fluffy white clouds. It was staggering, he knew. But it wasn't home. Nothing would ever persuade him that his modest house was in any way inferior to this.

And then that sleek black car came into view, and the lump in his stomach started to grow and curdle. Nicholas. He reached automatically for the gearstick, intending to stick the car straight in reverse and get out of there as quickly as possible. But Rachel turned towards him.

'Leo? What is it? You're shaking.'

'Maybe this is a bad idea. We could still go. It's not too late.'

But the front door opened, and he glimpsed

his mum standing inside, shielding her eyes from the low winter sun. He saw the moment when she realised that it was him in the car, because her face broke into a broad grin. And he hit the brakes.

He reached for Rachel's hand and held tight. 'Nicholas is here.'

'Still want to do this?' She stretched an arm across his shoulders, and drew herself closer.

He hesitated, but nodded. He couldn't leave now that his mum had seen him. Maybe it was better to get this done.

He glanced down at Rachel's belly, and re-alised that his mum would guess their news the second that they stepped out of the car. Per-haps this wasn't such a good idea. He should have spoken to his parents first, in private. Let them get used to the idea before he introduced Rachel. This probably wasn't fair on Rachel, either. Throwing her into the middle of his family dramas. But they were here now and there was no going back.

Rachel watched as all the colour drained from Leo's face, and he gripped the car door handle as if he never wanted to let go.

She walked around the front of the car and stopped in front of him. 'If you're sure you want to do this—' she laid a gentle hand over his white knuckles '—then let's go in. No point putting it off any more. And I think we owe your mum an explanation.' She'd seen the way the other woman's eyes had widened to take in her bump, and the blatant curiosity that had followed.

She tangled her fingers in his as he shut the car door and pocketed the keys, and squeezed his hand as they walked towards the door. His mum, a short, plump woman, with pink cheeks and brightly blonde hair, stood leaning against the door frame, her expression beaming pride and happiness.

'Hi, Mum. Happy birthday.' Leo's voice was solemn as he leaned in to kiss her on the cheek. 'This is Rachel. Rachel, this is my mum, Michelle. Mum, we have some news for you.'

Rachel flinched. It didn't exactly set the jubilant tone that news of a baby should bring.

She followed them through the house to the kitchen, suddenly feeling nervous and awkward, as Leo's mum called to the rest of the family. 'Francis, Nicholas, are you there? Leo's here and he has some news for us!'

Leo gripped her hand a little harder, and she squeezed back, letting him know that he wasn't doing this alone, that she would face down his brother with him.

When she looked up, Michelle was watching them expectantly.

'Right then, Rachel. Can I get you anything? Something to drink? Leo, are you hungry yet?'

'No, thanks.' Rachel tried to smile, but Leo's nerves were rubbing off on her, travelling up from his tight-gripped hand to make her shoulders tense, her posture awkward. Her belly was the elephant in the room while they waited for the family to gather in the kitchen.

Two men walked in through the door on the opposite side of the kitchen, and she thought that Leo might actually bolt. His whole body tensed and she looked up and saw fight or flight playing out on his features. His forehead was shining slightly and his limbs were stiff and tense, ready to run or strike. She wished she could reach out and hold him. She knew that facing his brother was painful for him, clearly almost unbearably so.

But he hadn't reached for her. And if that was what he wanted then surely he would.

'So what's this new—' Leo's father's voice boomed, before he caught sight of the bump and stopped mid-sentence.

Nicholas—or at least that was who she guessed he was; Leo wasn't exactly making introductions—sent her a charming smile from behind his father's back. She remembered what

Leo had said about how he used that charm, and sent a subtle scowl back.

'Leo?' his father prompted him, but Leo seemed frozen. Unable to move or speak.

Rachel stuck out her hand. 'I'm Rachel, a friend of Leo's,' she introduced herself. Using the movement to cover a quick squeeze to Leo's hand. His arm moved, and, just slightly, the rest of his body followed as he ushered her across the centre of the room towards his family.

'Rachel, this is Nicholas. My brother.'

'How do you do?' She forced the words out, though they felt rotten in her mouth. Well, this was awkward. She wished she'd known that Leo was going to freeze like this. She could hardly blame him, knowing everything that he'd gone through because of his brother. But at some point they had to spill the beans about this baby.

'So, this news…' Michelle prompted, her eyes flashing again to Rachel's bump.

She glanced up to Leo again, wondering whether he was going to step in—but no. He was no nearer composure than he had been before. They were facing things together, were stronger together. And if he needed her to, she would do this for the both of them.

She glanced up at him in a question, and he

nodded fractionally in response. All she really wanted to do was disappear with him for a few minutes, get the smile back on his face and his softness back in his body.

She forced a smile to her lips instead. 'We're expecting a baby,' she announced.

Michelle flew at her across the kitchen and wrapped her in a hug. 'That's wonderful news! Oh, a baby in the family. Brilliant.' Overwhelmed by this reaction, so much warmer than the one she'd received from her own mother, Rachel felt tears gathering in her eyes. There was nothing to worry about here. Until she looked over Michelle's shoulder and saw a knowing half-grin on Nicholas's face. She glanced up at Leo and realised that he was looking at his brother, too, eyes locked together with decades-old hostility. It was unbelievable his parents didn't know something was wrong.

'I've got so many questions,' Michelle said. 'When did you two meet? When's the baby due?' She must have spotted the conspiratorial glance that passed between Rachel and Leo, because she blushed, and moved the conversation swiftly on. 'But you can fill us in on all the details later. Let's just open a bottle of something fizzy now and celebrate.' When she turned to the fridge, Leo looked over at Rachel, and she gave his arm a quick squeeze.

His dad returned with a handful of champagne flutes, which he deposited on the worktop before clapping Leo into a hug, and kissing Rachel on the cheek.

'A baby. Marvellous news,' he declared. 'Don't you think so, Nick? You'll be an uncle, of course. Really wonderful news.'

Rachel eyed Nick carefully, trying to see the cruelty behind this affable exterior. And there it was. The slight lift of his eyebrow changed his smile to a smirk. It gave him a slight air of superiority, as if he had guessed exactly how planned this pregnancy was. She could practically see the X-rated guessing games playing across his brain. Pervert. Michelle handed her a cold flute of champagne and she took it, wishing she could gulp it down.

'To the new Fairfax,' Michelle toasted. And then stopped when she saw the look that Rachel threw at Leo—they definitely hadn't decided on a surname yet. 'And there's my foot in my mouth again. Here's to the new baby, whatever his or her name might be.'

'Cheers.' Rachel clinked glasses and allowed herself a sip of champagne, closing her eyes to savour the taste.

She kept an eye on Nick for the rest of the afternoon, as the family chatted in the kitchen while Francis cooked. Her heart ached for Leo, seeing how uncomfortable he was around his brother, and the selfless way he put his mother's feelings above his own by being here. But he wished he weren't—that much was evident from the way his body had grown more and more tense and his words more and more terse.

Michelle had noticed it, too, she realised: she became more watchful, glancing at Leo more and more often, though never drawing attention to it by asking him what was wrong. How long had she suspected? Rachel wondered. How long had she been aware of the fractures in her family without knowing the cause?

Rachel could see that Nick's accusations about Michelle being a gold-digger were unfounded. The mutual adoration between Leo's parents was clear to anyone who cared to see it. Perhaps jealousy was the root of all Nick's behaviour. It couldn't have been easy to see his mother replaced so fully in his father's affections. But to take that out on his innocent brother was inexcusable. Was it unforgivable, as well? Was there any way back from animosity for these brothers? But she wasn't so naive that she thought that she could bring about a reconciliation.

By the time they sat down to dinner, her shoulders had followed Leo's, fixed into a stiff line. It was impossible to relax with Leo tense beside her, and she felt every moment of his discomfort with him. His parents were smiling and upbeat, but they weren't as oblivious to the tension between the brothers as Leo had told her they were.

Her moment of relief when dinner was finished vanished in the second when Michelle casually suggested, 'You boys will sort out the kitchen, won't you? It will give you a chance to catch up. And your father and me a chance to interrogate this lovely young woman.' Her horror at the prospect of Leo being stuck alone with Nick must have shown, but fortunately was misinterpreted. 'I was only joking, Rachel, lovey. Absolutely no embarrassing questions.' She shoved a stack of empty plates into Leo's hands, giving him no choice but to take them through to the kitchen.

Rachel tried to follow Michelle's questions while keeping half an ear out for signs of physical altercation in the kitchen. She told her about due dates and scans, and a highly edited version of how she and Leo had met, and then spotted a couple of empty wine and water bottles on a side table. She stood abruptly, grabbed the bottles and headed for the door, brushing off Michelle's protestations that she wasn't to help.

She slowed as she approached the kitchen door, expecting to hear raised voices. But it was ominously quiet. She paused before she pushed it open, and heard the low murmurs and hisses of men who didn't want to be overheard. But not so quiet that she couldn't hear what they were saying.

Nick's voice, low and vindictive: 'She's after your money, is that it? Can't think why else she'd be interested. Maybe she heard that your mother slept her way into a nice house and a fat bank account and thought she'd try the same. Or maybe you cooked it up between you. A way to get a bigger slice of Dad's inheritance.'

'Don't you dare speak about Rachel that way.' Leo's voice was a hiss. 'Or Mum. After all these years can you still not see—' She could hear the venom packed into the tight syllables, the years of hatred he was trying to keep from spilling out into a shout.

'But maybe the little bastard isn't even yours. She wouldn't be entitled to a penny then. You'll be getting a paternity test, I assume. Stupid not to with a girl like that.'

Through the crack in the door she saw Leo's hand tighten into a fist. She opened the door with a bang and strode into the room, shoving the bottles on the worktop and turning to Nick with a scowl.

'Actually there was no need. But obviously we're grateful for your concern for your new niece or nephew.'

'Rachel, stay out of this,' Leo hissed. 'I'm handling it.' Turning to his brother, Leo spoke with low menace.

'Apologise. Now.'

But she didn't need him to fight her battles for her. Nick had been allowed to get away with bullying for years, and she had no interest in being his next victim. 'I think it was Nick who involved me, Leo. Is there anything else you'd like to know about my personal life, Nick? Because you obviously think who I sleep with is your business. Perhaps you want to see my medical notes and employment history. Or are facts less fun than snide accusations?'

'Rachel…' After just one word his voice had slipped into the smooth honey of a serial liar, using practised charm to cover his misdeeds. Good job she was much too smart, and too angry, to fall for it. 'I don't know what you think you heard—'

'You know what you said, you bastard. Now apologise.'

'Bastard?' Nicholas raised a mocking eyebrow at Leo. 'I hardly think your little family is in a position to throw stones.'

'That's enough!' Rachel looked at Leo in

shock. She had never heard him raise his voice before. He'd always wielded quiet authority and humour to get what he wanted, without needing to shout about it.

'What's going on here? Boys?'

Rachel turned on the spot, to find Michelle and Francis behind her.

'It's nothing, Mum,' Leo said, painting on a smile that would convince no one. 'We were just on our way back.'

'It didn't sound like nothing; it sounded to us as if Nick said something to upset Rachel. Nick?'

He smiled, smirked, and raised his palms in innocence. 'A complete misunderstanding. Hormo—'

She saw anger flash again in Leo's eyes, and his fist reach back. She grabbed his hand and threw him a warning look. The last thing this situation needed was to escalate into violence.

'Finish that word and you'll live to regret it.' Even as she said the words, she was aware of the damage that she was doing, that Leo had tried for years to keep the family oblivious to the problems at the heart of it, and here she was hanging out dirty laundry for anyone to see. But Nick had bullied and intimidated for too long. She wasn't a scared child and she wouldn't stand for it.

She locked eyes with Nick, refusing to be the first to look away. She didn't want him thinking he could cow her, that she would back down from him as she was sure that many others had done in the past. She was at an advantage—had known his capacity for malice before even meeting him—and she had no intention of falling for his charming shtick.

Leo's voice broke the heavy silence. 'Mum, I'm sorry but I think we need to be going. Don't worry. Everything's fine.'

'But, Leo,' Michelle protested. 'There's something you're all hiding and I don't like it. We should talk about this.'

'It's between me and Nick. It wasn't fair of us to bring it up now and spoil your birthday. We'll sort it out another time.'

'Rachel?'

She hesitated, wanting to help. Leo was allowing Nick to drive a wedge into the heart of the family. However much he thought he was helping his mum, he wasn't hiding from her the fact that something was wrong. But it wasn't her story to tell—the most she could do was be there for Leo when he decided it was the right time.

'I think we should go, Michelle. But it's been so lovely meeting you. And I'll speak to you soon. I'll email you the pictures from the scan.'

'It's been lovely meeting you, too,' Leo's mum replied, though the wary look she gave her sons told them all she wasn't happy about them leaving before this was sorted. 'I can't tell you how excited we are about the baby. And you being part of the family, of course.'

Leo hustled her out of the house so quickly she barely had a chance to kiss Francis on the cheek and throw Nicholas an 'I know your game' glare.

The silence in the car was thick and heavy, and lasted for far longer than Rachel liked. Past cross, past angry and heading to furious. With every minute that went by with Leo not saying a word, the dread in her belly grew thicker and the chance of the day ending without another argument disappeared.

They sat in silence for a moment longer after the car pulled up outside the house. And Rachel wondered what Leo was working up to. She could see from his white knuckles on the steering wheel and the solid tension from left fingertip to right, through the stiff lines of his arms and shoulders, that it was something big.

He was angry. And although she knew how much he hated his brother and how angry he was at him, she also knew he was mad at her. She'd told herself on the drive back that the reason his eyes had been fixed so determinedly on the road was an overzealous adherence to the Highway Code. But the fact that his eyes remained fixed through the windscreen, even now they were stationary, confirmed her worst fear. He couldn't even look at her. Perhaps she had been rash confronting Nick like that, when she knew how much history there was between Leo and his brother. And how Leo had kept their problems secret from the rest of the family for years. But was she meant to ignore it? Let Nick get away with hurting and provoking Leo, because that was what he always did? Perhaps. It was what Leo had wanted. He'd never asked her to jump to his defence. But when someone hurt him, it hurt her. It hurt their family, and she hadn't been able to stand it.

'I'm sorry.' She reached out a hand and brushed it against Leo's, hoping to soften the tension there. But he flinched away from her. She caught her breath, shocked by the pain his rejection had caused in her chest. 'I didn't mean to cause a scene.'

'Well, you still did a good job of it. You know I didn't want my parents to find out about the problems between me and Nick. I don't want them to have to deal with our issues. You knew that and yet you went ahead anyway.'

'How was I supposed to let him say those

things about you and me—and let him get away with it?'

'I wasn't going to let him get away with it.' He turned to face her now, and his rage showed in his every feature, his skin flushed, his forehead lined, his mouth thin and hard. He had retreated to the far side of the car, arms crossed again, putting every distance and barrier he could between them again. She was desperate to reach out to him, to feel his arms wrapped around her as they had just a few hours ago. 'There are ways of dealing with this that don't involve my parents.'

'Yes, and those ways have led to you suffering in silence for years. I couldn't add to that, couldn't stand by and watch you hurting. Again.'

'I told you not to interfere, Rachel. It's not worth tearing my family apart for. However much he may have dented your ego.'

'It's not about my ego, Leo.' Her voice was raised now, too, frustrated that he thought this all came down to her wanting to defend her reputation. It was nothing to do with her. She wanted to defend Leo. To protect him. 'He can say what he likes about me. I don't care about his opinion. But I won't let him get away with bullying. And I can't believe you think your parents don't know what's going on. Are you really that blind? They must have known for years if that's how you normally behave when you're at home. Your mother watches you like a hawk. If you'd just talk to them—'

'And say what? My brother bullied me when we were children. He made me miserable, and I avoid seeing you if it means seeing him. There is no easy solution to this, Rachel. I don't want to have to make my parents choose. Can't fix this on a schedule. I'm sorry that my family won't bend to what you want.'

'That's not what I was trying to do, Leo.' The heat went out of her voice, as she realised how badly Leo had misunderstood her, how big a hole she had dug for them. 'I've apologised for being rash. He was rude; I pulled him up on it. That's all.'

'That's enough! That's enough to keep Nick happy, for him to be satisfied that he's got to me again. I specifically told you that I didn't want a confrontation. What happened is in the past, and I want it to stay there. I'm happy with how I've moved on, and I don't need to relive the worst years of my life just because you want to play happy families. Especially when your own family is so messed up. You think you can come to my parents' home and dig up issues that have been dealt with, but you can't even face your own problems. Can't tell your parents that they've suffocated you with their overprotection. That you're crippled because of the way they have treated you.'

His words hit her like a slap, and she sucked in a breath, tried to recover from their sting. All she had done was try to help him, and he threw her own failed family life back in her face. 'I—'

'You trapped me,' he said. 'And now there's nothing I can do. I can never be free of you.'

She counted to ten very, *very* slowly, reminding herself that murdering the father of her unborn child was in nobody's best interest.

'We're obviously both emotional. I think we need to cool down and talk about this tomorrow. Let's just go to bed and get some sleep.'

She reached for the door handle but turned back when she realised Leo hadn't moved. 'Aren't you coming inside?'

'I don't think I'm going to want to talk about this tomorrow.'

She sighed. 'We'll talk about it tonight, then, if that's what you want. But either way you're going to have to get out of the car.'

She let out a relieved breath when he finally let go, and turned to look at her.

But when his eyes met hers, she wished she'd let him sit there a little longer. Because what she saw made the dread she'd felt earlier seem like the lightest of butterflies. What she felt now was a lead anvil, heavy despair just waiting to crush her.

'I don't want to talk about it tonight. I don't want to talk about it tomorrow. Rachel, I don't want to talk about this at all. I realised something, driving back here. We've both made a mess of our family lives. And still we think we're doing the right thing creating a new family out of two people who barely know each other and have nothing more in common than an ill-advised night in bed together. We're making a mistake.'

'Leo, I don't understand.' Tears broke her voice, but she forced words out anyway, trying to find a way to fix this. 'What mistake?'

'This!' A sharp, sweeping hand movement took in the two of them.

'You've changed your mind about the baby. About wanting to be involved?'

'No. Not about that. I want this baby. I want to be a good father. But I don't want to do it like this. With you and me playing happy families. It's impossible. We have to face facts.'

She pushed open the car door and shambled out onto the path, not wanting to believe what she was hearing. She'd spent six months redrawing her picture of her life, trying to see the shapes and contours and details of her future. In the last weeks, she'd finally started to understand it. To see the picture emerging from the chaos. To push the fragments of her old life into this new scenario with Leo and the baby and make sense of it all. And in the last days she'd felt the pleasure and delights of falling into bed with him, of feeling his arms around her, and knowing that whatever big, scary, overwhelming emotions she'd felt in the past six months, he returned them. He felt for her as much as she did for him.

And that was what was driving the knife of hurt into her chest. The complete corruption of her life plans was nothing compared to the pain of him pushing her away. That not only did he not love her, he wasn't even interested in trying. She pushed away from the car, stumbling slightly as she headed up the path. She wasn't even sure where she was going; all she knew was that she had to get away from him.

She wrapped her arms around her belly, protecting her baby from his harsh words and her own hurt. He was just striking out because he had seen his brother. She stopped for a moment and almost walked back. And then she saw the hard, uncompromising expression he wore and hesitated. But they were expecting a child. They couldn't just give up. She took another step back to the car and spoke. 'Leo, please. I don't believe that you can just walk away—'

He climbed out of the car and leant against it, keeping the hulk of metal between them. 'And that was what you wanted all along, wasn't it? Me completely unable to walk away from this. Trapped. No way out. You planned it.'

His words struck her like arrows. The injustice biting at her. Each word's sting sharper than the last.

'I—'

'I can never be free of you.'

It wasn't the words that hurt the most; it was the expression on his face. The pain, fear and resignation that told her he meant every one of them. He was broken, afraid and angry—and he blamed her entirely. She walked to the door, grabbed the spare key from beneath a plant pot and let herself in, not looking back to see whether Leo was following her. Upstairs, she swept her clothes from a drawer with one hand while ordering a cab from her smartphone with the other. By the time she returned to the front door, packed and ready to go, she'd already had a text to tell her the car was on the way.

She took a deep breath, steeling herself to see Leo.

She couldn't believe that he'd accused her of trapping him on purpose. Couldn't believe that this man, with whom she'd felt so close just a few hours before, could believe her capable of deceiving him. No crappy childhood made it okay to treat her like that.

He wasn't in the house. She'd listened for him when she'd left the guest room, not quite sure whether she wanted him to be there or not. But as she'd tiptoed through the cottage it had become clear to her that there was no need to be quiet. He wasn't there. When she opened the front door, the car was still there. Doors closed and locked, with no sign of Leo.

He must have walked down to the beach, she surmised. Either to walk by the water or work in his studio. She considered walking down there to find him. But even if the prospect of walking down an uneven and unlit coastal path at night while six months pregnant hadn't seemed like a stupid idea, she wouldn't have gone. Why should she chase after him, after what he had said to her? Why should she give him the courtesy of letting him know that she was going, when he could stand there and accuse her of lying to him, of deliberately getting pregnant? Of manipulating him.

As she looked out of the front door, her taxi pulled up. And with one last look down the path to the beach, she opened the door and slipped inside.

* * *

Leo laid his hands flat on his workbench and let out a long breath. His skin felt tight and itchy, as though it were too small for his body. He'd watched Rachel walk into his house and shut the door and then suddenly it had seemed impossible to stay still. Adrenaline had flooded his body and demanded that he move.

He'd stalked off at a tearing pace down the path to the beach, not knowing why he was going, where he was going. And already regretting his words to Rachel. But he had felt trapped in the situation and in that second he had hated it. It didn't matter whether he would choose to be with her, whether if circumstances had been different they could have found a way to be together. All that mattered was that the baby had locked them together for life, and he'd had no choice about it. About any of it. It had seemed so important, in that moment, to have a choice about something. To control the nature of their relationship, now that he knew that she would be in his life for ever. Even if it meant hurting Rachel, hurting himself, in the process.

He held on to the bench, trying to anchor himself, trying to suppress the energy coursing through his muscles, forcing him to keep moving. He grabbed a block of wood and a file and started hacking away at it, willing some form to emerge. Some shape or texture to distract him from the tempest in his mind.

It wouldn't come. Of course it wouldn't. He was in no mood to create. His body was so filled with rage and sadness and regret that he could barely make his hands move where he wanted them, never mind let them find beauty in something.

He threw the block of wood down, angry with himself for the waste of something that had so much potential, and which had been sacrificed for no reason other than that he couldn't think of any other way to rid himself of these overwhelming emotions.

Where could they go from here? He'd told Rachel that they were making a mistake. That they shouldn't try to be a family. But this baby was coming, and he'd not for a second wished it weren't. This wasn't about the baby. His heart still felt a little fuller, his spine a little straighter and the corners of his mouth a little higher when he thought about his child growing inside Rachel. He could not and would not walk away from his responsibilities as a father.

That wasn't what scared him. It wasn't the prospect of being a father that had made him panic—that had made him feel as if the structure of the car were closing in on him, as if he'd inadvertently driven into a crusher at a scrapyard.

It was the prospect of a lifetime with Rachel. Because however much they might tell themselves that they didn't need to make decisions like that now, however much they thought that they could take things slow, like other people, date, get to know one another, find out what these feelings they had for one another meant, this situation was different. In their lives, you didn't get to walk away if things became hard. If she hurt him—if she betrayed him—he would still have to endure a life with her in it, and he wasn't sure that he could bear that.

And how could he know that she wouldn't hurt him? He'd thought he was safe, once. Thought that as long as he had people around him that loved him, he would be okay. When the bullying had started at school, he'd told himself that it would be all right. That his brother would look out for him. That his dad would intervene if it got too bad.

And the day that he'd found out that Nick was at the heart of his being tormented, his faith in family, and trust, and love, had shattered. If he couldn't trust his own brother not to hurt him, then how could he ever trust anyone else?

He could never trust her. And if he couldn't

trust her, they'd never be happy. They were best off acknowledging that now. Trying to find a way to get along with neither of them getting involved emotionally. With neither of them getting hurt.

He'd got too close already.

He glanced out of the window, saw that the fingers of light that were still tinting the sky pink when he'd left the car had long left the beach, which was now pitch dark. The stars and moon were eerily bright and reflected in the still, flat sea. He locked up the workshop, faltering over the action, stretching out the task, unwilling to return to the house. Would she be there? He didn't deserve for her to be, that was sure. He didn't even know if he wanted her to be.

But he wanted her. That much was true. He wanted to lose himself in her body. Comfort himself with her nearness and warmth. To bury his face in her hair and forget about the world. To enjoy her just for now without having to think about tomorrow. It wasn't fair, it wasn't right. But it was the only thing he could think of that would ease the ache in his chest.

CHAPTER ELEVEN

TAP-TAP-TAP. Tap-tap-tap-tap.

Rachel hit the end of her pencil on her desk as she scrolled through her inbox, trying to locate the email she needed. She knew it was here somewhere. She just needed to focus. But there was the problem. With her personal life in chaos, it was impossible to concentrate.

She needed to fix it. Any other problem in her life she considered the options, found the best solution, implemented it. Christmas had come and gone with barely more than a text from Leo, leaving a heavy lead feeling in her belly, somewhere low and hard to hide from. Leo had apologised for his harsh words. For the fact she'd felt she had to leave. But there was more to say. The days were crawling by in a grey fog, and she'd had enough of the uncertainty. She couldn't begin the new year sitting doing nothing, not knowing. She wanted answers, and she'd have to go and get them.

The office would be closed for the weekend and bank holiday, giving her the perfect break in her schedule.

The shrill sound of her mobile grabbed her attention, and she groaned as she glanced at the screen. Mum.

Christmas with her parents, the first time she'd spent more than a day with them since she'd met Leo, had been something of a challenge. Far from the unquestioning support she'd hoped for from her mum and dad, every conversation about the baby had been so full of doubts and worries that she'd found herself driven crazy before the end of Boxing Day. And now, no doubt, her mother was calling to ask her—again—if she was sure that she wouldn't come to them for the new year. She should be taking it easy, she'd been told a thousand times in the last week. Shouldn't be out partying with her friends, or schlepping down to Dorset. She should be at home where she could be looked after—wrapped in cotton wool and stifled till she couldn't breathe, more like.

She took a deep breath and hit answer, preparing for another heavy round.

'Hi, Mum.'

She rubbed the heel of her hand against her forehead as she listened to her mother repeat everything she'd heard over Christmas. Get lots of rest…we'll be able to look after you… won't have to lift a finger…London so unpleasant on New Year's Eve.

For a moment, she considered telling her that she wasn't planning on being *in* London for the rest of the day, but somehow she didn't think that the idea of her getting on a train down to Dorset was going to do her mum's nerves any favours.

Eventually, when her mum had exhausted all possible worries for that weekend, she turned the subject to her current favourite: asking Rachel to reconsider having her come and stay after the birth.

'I really think that it would be best, darling. I know that Leo wants to be there, but what does he know about babies? There are so many risks in those early days. So much to learn. Keeping the temperature moderated, getting those feeds done right. And if something goes wrong…have you seen the statistics of sudden infant deaths?'

'Mum, that's enough.'

Rachel found that she was standing at her desk, having stood up on impulse. Her mum was only worried. But her worrying was so far over the top it was unbelievable. And the last thing that Rachel needed in order to be a calm, capable mum herself was scaremongering.

'Leo and I have made a decision together, and you're going to have to accept it. Of course we'd love you to visit. But this is our child, our decision, and you're going to have to let us make our own mistakes. All these years you've been trying to protect me, it's made things worse. Made it so that I can't recognise which dangers are real and which I've created. I won't go on that way, and I won't have my child growing up as afraid as I am.'

She sat back down, and concentrated on softening her voice as she spoke again. Her mum's shocked silence on the other end of the phone spoke volumes, and Rachel felt guilty, knowing her mum had only ever wanted what was best for her.

'I'm sorry, Mum, I didn't mean to shout. But you have to let me do this my way.'

There was another long silence at the end of the phone, and then a sniff. But Rachel held her ground, knowing that she had to stand by her words if she wanted this relationship to work. Eventually, her mum spoke. 'I'm sorry, darling. I didn't know you felt that way. We've only ever wanted...'

'What's best for me. I know.' Rachel breathed a long sigh, relieved that her mum was still talking to her, and more importantly could see her point of view. 'But really, truthfully, Mum, what's best for me is letting me make my own mistakes, my own decisions. And trusting me to know what I want.' After a few more minutes, Rachel made her excuses, knowing that if she was going to get down to Dorset she would have to head off soon.

She looked back at her emails, and finally found the one she'd drafted to Leo, letting him know she was coming. She'd held off sending it, not sure whether warning him was the best thing to do. Because giving each other time to think about what they were going to say to each other wasn't working so well right now. Leo had retreated into a polite, distant, paler version of the man she'd known. Sending careful words over email and text, not the funny, impulsive, challenging humour she'd grown to love. And the only way she could think of to shake them out of this stalemate was to turn up at his place and have it out with him. She hovered over Send, before making up her mind. Better just to turn up. She hit Delete instead and shut down her computer.

Pulling on a scarf and fleece-lined gloves, she approached the revolving doors to the street, using her teeth to pull on the second glove—why did no one warn you about the third-trimester swollen fingers? Juggling the handle of her wheeled case and lifting the strap of her handbag over her head, she pulled harder on the glove, and nearly lost her balance when she walked straight into something tall and solid.

She swayed, trying to re-find her centre of gravity, not as easy as it used to be, but a big, heavy hand found the middle of her back and held steady until she got her footing.

She drank in his damp hair, the heavy wool coat and the familiar blue sparkle of his eyes. For the past few weeks she'd been convinced that he never wanted to talk to her again. And given the way they'd left things, if they weren't expecting a child together her wounded pride might have tempted her to leave things that way. She'd thought that it would be a challenge even getting him to speak to her tonight. Now he was at her office, wearing an open expression and a tentative smile, and she had no idea what to make of it.

But, what if he wasn't here to see her? She felt a little flush of colour rising on her neck as she remembered the last time he'd surprised her at her office. She'd mistakenly jumped to the conclusion then that he was here to see her, and she wouldn't make the same mistake twice. Wouldn't show her cards before she knew what he wanted. There had been enough humiliation and hurt.

'Leo? What are you doing here?'

'What do you think? I'm here to see you. To apologise for…for the last time I saw you. And to show you something. Something important.'

There was a time that knowing he wanted to see her would have started a fizz of desire and anticipation. Today, there was too much still standing between them, too much doubt and distrust weighing on her emotions. Seeing him still halted her breath in her throat, made her want to reach for him, but when she didn't know what she wanted from him, what she wanted for herself, then she couldn't know if that was a good thing.

He glanced down at her case. 'Going somewhere?'

She dropped the handle, had almost forgotten she was holding it. For a split second, she thought about lying. But what would be the point? Ten minutes ago she was set on going to see him to talk things through. What good would chickening out now do?

'To see you, actually.'

His face broke into a full smile, lips turned up, eyes twinkling, cheeks creasing into fine lines with the breadth of his grin. She remembered all the times one of these full-wattage smiles had created a mirror image on her own face. Today, it made her shoulders tense. He was practically bouncing now, exuding barely repressed energy. He was so different from the silent, icy man she had left seething in his car, and the change in him was unsettling. She had been prepared to do battle with taciturnity and now he was grinning at her. What had happened?

'I was coming to talk,' she told him, keeping her voice carefully neutral. 'We can't leave things like we did last time. There's too much at stake. Too much for us to decide.'

'Absolutely.' His expression turned serious, but the sparkle didn't leave his eyes. 'There's so much I want to say. I wasn't sure whether you'd listen.'

She glanced around her. People were still milling about in Reception, the atmosphere festive and full of anticipation.

'Okay, but I don't want to do this here.'

Rachel lowered herself onto her couch, letting out an involuntary sigh of relief as the weight left her feet.

'Long day?' Leo asked, dropping beside her.

'They're all feeling long lately.'

His eyes held hers for long moments, and as she watched they softened from frantic energy to something gentler and more intimate. 'Were you really coming down to my place?'

She nodded and looked away. His gaze was too intense; he saw too much.

'You wanted to talk?'

'I think there's a lot we need to say.' She shifted on the couch, trying to get comfortable. She shoved a cushion or two behind her back to combat the ache there, but they pushed her closer to Leo. She could have moved to the armchair, or could have asked him to move. But sitting close to him was making her body glow in ways she'd forgotten about in the past few weeks, drowned out by the hurt of his words and withdrawal. She stayed put, telling herself that as long as they weren't actually touching, then she was in no danger.

She focused inwards, trying to block out the quickening of her pulse, the way his scent was tickling at her senses. Eventually she spoke, repeating the words she'd rehearsed before she'd left for work that morning. 'Leo, we need to talk about what we're going to do. How you want to be involved with your child. We can't go on like the last few weeks.'

She'd thought long and hard about what she was going to say to him. Whether pushing him to talk was the right thing to do. But Nicholas Fairfax had been allowed to get away with too much for too long. She wasn't going to let him ruin her life from a distance without fighting for what she wanted. And she'd sworn she couldn't walk away from the wreckage of her and Leo until the ashes were cold and there was no hope of them reigniting. Now, faced with a Leo so different from the man she'd last seen, her carefully thought-out plan didn't seem to apply. No change there, then.

'I need to apologise. I know I've already said it, but I need you to understand how sorry I am for what I said. I should never have attacked you, or your family, like that, and I'm sorry. I don't think we're making a mistake, having this baby, and I think that we can be wonderful parents.'

She was so shocked by this speech that it took her a few moments to gather her thoughts and translate them into words.

'Thank you for apologising.' She had to stop a sigh of relief escaping her lips as he spoke. She had told herself ever since that horrendous afternoon that he had been lashing out because seeing his brother had brought up more bad memories than he could handle. But deep down she'd wondered if that was all there was to it. Whether seeing his family had merely provided the excuse that he'd been looking for to escape from her and their child. The future that they promised.

But seeing Leo here, looking happy and

open in a way she'd never quite seen him before, she felt as if her worst fears were quietened, and she let herself hope, for the first time, that they could find a way back to that steamy night after the gala, the intimacy and tenderness they'd shared that night in his house by the sea.

'I'm sorry, too, Leo.' Because the blame wasn't all his. The way that she had interfered with his family, when he'd specifically asked her not to, had played on her mind since that afternoon. If she'd gone into that confrontation less determined to make Nick pay for what he'd done, had helped Leo, rather than forcing the issue, then they could have found a way to change things without reaching breaking point. 'I made things worse with Nick.'

Leo shook his head.

'No, you did exactly the right thing.'

She wished that she could believe him, but that hadn't been what he'd said when he'd left her alone in a dark, cold house, and told her that he didn't believe in their new family.

'I don't understand…'

'Nick. I should have faced him down years ago. You were right about my parents. They knew something was wrong. I went home for Christmas. Ignored Nick's usual behaviour on Christmas Day, Boxing Day. And then I couldn't take it any more. I thought about the way that you faced him. How you pulled him up on his insinuations and snide remarks and decided that he shouldn't get away with it. I confronted him and my parents practically applauded.'

Rachel smiled, imagining the scene, unbelievably proud of Leo for doing the one thing he'd feared most. 'That's brilliant, Leo. I'm so glad you were able to talk to your parents about things.'

'But that's not all.' He reached across the sofa for her hand, gripped her fingers and pulled her a little closer to him. 'After I'd done it, all I could think about was how I'd let you down. How I'd let Nick get to me until I barely knew what I was saying. I'd let him spoil what we had, and I had to fix it. I want you back, Rachel.'

'Leo…' The change in him was so obvious that there was no point disputing that his confrontation with his brother had resolved so many of his issues. But Leo suddenly deciding that he wanted to try again wouldn't be enough to make this relationship work. Maybe he'd been right. They were crazy to think that they could just try and mash their two lives together and think that they could make a family from it. 'I'm really pleased things are better with your family. But I don't think that us as a couple is going to work.'

'Don't you want it? Because I can promise you I've never wanted anything more. I know that I can't fix this overnight. I know that it will take time to trust again, but I want to work at this. I want to deserve you again.'

'I want it, too.' She could never say otherwise. How could she when her body craved his, when she missed the way that he made her laugh, relax, be the version of herself that wasn't constantly afraid of something going wrong? 'It's just not that simple, Leo.'

'I know it's not simple,' he called over his shoulder as he reached into the holdall he'd thrown on the floor earlier. 'Trust me, I know that. But it's not impossible. If we want to try, we *can* do this. And I can prove it.'

He turned back to her with a boyish grin, and held out a dog-eared sketch pad. On the front, in a hand-drawn cursive script, were the words 'Archer Fairfax Family'.

She looked up at him in surprise. 'Leo? What's—'

'It's a plan!' The boyish excitement was back, and he bounced the sofa cushions with his energy. She laughed in response—it was contagious. 'Not a plan for everything. But what we agreed, a compromise. A plan for the big stuff, the stuff we have to decide in advance. The rest of it we explore as we go along.'

Stunned into silence, she opened the cover and flicked through the first pages. Like the plans she'd once seen on his kitchen table, they were beautiful. Sketched line drawings and scatterings of bullet points and script. His house. Her flat. A baby swaddled in blankets. From the pictures, and a scattering of jottings, a picture of their lives started to emerge. Living together in her flat in London, the baby in a cot by their bed. In the city in the week, close to her work with rented studio space for Leo. Weekends at the coast. The three of them looking out to sea.

She laid the pad in her lap, resting her hands on it, tracing the lines of the sea with a finger.

'You think we can do this?'

'I do. I love you, Rachel. I love the way you laugh, and the way you are so utterly unfazed by the most terrifying things I can think of. I love that you stood up to my idiot brother. I love that you've been an incredible mother to our child before he—or she—is even here. The past few weeks, not speaking to you, have been the worst that I can remember. I think we already know how to do this; we've just been fending for ourselves for so long that we have to remember how to let someone else in.'

'And you'd do it? You'd live in the city?' The sea, the beach, his workshop were so much a part of who he was she couldn't imagine him without them. Would she be enough to make him happy? Could he be content with her?

'I'd live with you, if you'll have me. City, sea—we can do both. As long as we're together.'

'But your studio…'

'Is not as important to me as you are. There's studio space in London. Your office is here—it makes more sense for me to move. And the house isn't going anywhere. Weekends, holidays by the sea. It's the best of both worlds.'

She was still staring, she knew. But she could hardly let herself believe this: it was so far from what she had been expecting. Leo was still grinning at her, and her lips turned up in response.

'Tell me you feel the same. Tell me you want to try.'

'I don't know what to say, Leo. Last time I saw you…'

'Last time you saw me was the worst day of my life. I was angry and scared, and when I realised that you'd gone, that I'd driven you away, I was heartbroken. I swore to myself that

I would never let that happen again. That's why I went home for Christmas and faced my nasty little bully of a brother. And that's why I'm here, begging you to give us another chance.'

She glanced down again at the sketchbook, the image of the two of them, arms entwined around each other's bodies, looking out to sea with their baby safe between them. It was everything she wanted. He was everything she wanted.

From the minute she'd met him, she'd been rewriting the plan for her life, rethinking her future. For months it had been a hazy mass of maybes and what-ifs, but now she knew, without doubt, what she wanted. She wanted him, with all the surprises and madness that he brought her. For the way that he made her laugh, made her take risks, made them a family.

She reached up, and cupped his face in her hand. Drawing him close, she pressed a soft kiss to his lips. 'I love you, Leo. And you're right, I know we can do this. It's going to be terrifying and thrilling, and—at times—it's going to be downright confrontational. Which sounds to me like just about every other family on the planet. But you're going to make me happy, every day, even when you make me exasperated; and I promise I'm going to spend the rest of my life trying to make you happy, too.'

With his hand tangled in her hair, he kissed her back, wrapping his arm around her until he had his whole little family, his whole world, where he wanted them.

EPILOGUE

LOOK UP.

Rachel leaned against the bathroom door frame, watching Leo sprawled out on the bed. A tray of toast and coffee lay on the duvet beside him, and she had to fight the déjà vu. Nine months ago, she'd stood in this exact spot, and held her breath when she'd seen Leo still in her bed long after she'd thought he'd gone. This morning the picture was almost identical, apart from the precious bundle tucked into the crook of Leo's arm.

Their daughter. Three days old, and already the centre around which their whole world revolved.

Suddenly, Leo looked up and caught her eye. His face broke into a vast grin, his eyes shining; still with that disbelieving expression they'd both worn since the midwife had placed the baby on her chest and announced that they had a daughter.

She moved the tray to her bedside table, and slipped into the bed beside her lover and their baby girl, and breathed a sigh of contentment as she curled under Leo's other arm. 'Is this real?' she asked, looking up at him.

'I hope so, because I'm not letting her go. Or you.' Leo gazed from her to their daughter, his eyes still dreamy.

As Rachel reached across for the toast, her eye was caught by the corner of a sketch pad peeking out from under the bed. Just one of the many things she was getting used to since Leo had moved in: the propensity of belongings to show up anywhere and everywhere. That first morning, it would have driven her mad. Today it made her smile, evidence all around her of her new life, her new family.

She pulled the sketch pad up beside them and leafed through the familiar pictures as she ate her breakfast, lingering on the picture of them looking out to sea, the image that had spoken to her heart the day Leo had turned up asking her to trust him, to love him.

There were new pictures since then; she'd seen Leo scribbling away in the evenings as she'd scrolled through spreadsheets and handed over the final projects at work. There were sketches of her, her vast belly, her sleeping—or trying to. And over the past three days the most precious drawings of all. Their daughter's first hours. The first time she'd nursed, the first time she'd snuggled up in her Moses basket beside their bed. Her face screwed up with tears.

As she turned the page again, she started with surprise. A piece of paper had been pasted in. A drawing not of her or the baby. But of a hollow circle of wood, the grain spinning around the outside and through the centre. Her forehead creased as she turned the book through ninety degrees, trying to see where this picture fitted into the story. A new sculpture Leo was working on, perhaps, pasted into the wrong book? But when she turned the page, there it was again. The grain slightly different this time, more delicate. And the dimensions were different, too. The outer circle slightly narrower, the space inside larger.

When she turned the page again, the same image greeted her. This time with scribbled dimensions in millimetres, and fractions of millimetres, and something sparkling and glinting at the very top of the arch.

She dropped the book.

It was a sculpture, or a plan for one. A tiny sculpture, about the size of…

She looked up at Leo in surprise. 'A ring?'

He smiled down at her, shuffling the baby

in his arms as he reached under the duvet and pulled out a small wooden box, carved with a question mark on top, and unmistakably Leo's work.

As he handed it to her, she held his gaze, looking long and intensely into his eyes, trying to calm the galloping of her pulse and the hitches in her breathing. The box was smooth and warm in her hand, and she took a moment to trace the inscription on the lid with the pad of her finger.

She opened it slowly, pulling her eyes away from Leo's now, a smile playing at the corner of her lips.

A diamond gleamed at her, nestling in the wood-grained platinum as her antique bottle had nestled in the sand.

'Leo, it's beautiful.' She was so taken aback by its delicate beauty that for a moment its greater significance was lost on her. All her brain could process was the care and attention put into this exquisite item. Until Leo reached for her left hand, and pulled it towards him.

'Rachel, you've already made me happier and luckier than any man alive deserves to be. And I want you for ever. Will you be my wife?'

She grabbed his hand harder and hauled herself up on the bed until she was kneeling in front of him.

'Yes, Leo. Of course, yes. I love you. I will always love you, and everything you've given me, and I can't wait to spend the rest of my life with you.' She slipped the ring onto her finger, lifted the baby out of Leo's arms and into her basket, and leaned over to kiss her fiancé.

* * * * *

COMING NEXT MONTH FROM

HARLEQUIN

Romance

Available June 2, 2015

#4475 HIS UNEXPECTED BABY BOMBSHELL
by Soraya Lane

Best friends Rebecca and Ben were the couple most likely to marry, but when their chemistry finally bubbled over, it was on the night Ben left to become an international polo player. Now he's back, and Rebecca must tell Ben he's a father!

#4476 FALLING FOR THE BRIDESMAID
Summer Weddings • by Sophie Pembroke

Violet Huntingdon-Cross is always the bridesmaid, but could journalist Tom be the one she's been waiting for? As Tom helps her discover that love isn't just something that happens to other people, will falling for each other lead them down the aisle?

#4477 A MILLIONAIRE FOR CINDERELLA
In Love with the Boss • by Barbara Wallace

Patience Rush doesn't need a knight in shining armor. She's perfectly happy working as a housekeeper...until Stuart Duchenko arrives. He knows she's hiding something, but what? As they grow closer, Patience realizes that letting go of her past is the only way to a blissful future with Stuart...

#4478 FROM PARADISE...TO PREGNANT!
by Kandy Shepherd

A week in Bali was Zoe's dream vacation—until the island is hit by an earthquake! Trapped alongside high school crush Mitch, they seek comfort in each other's arms... But Zoe soon discovers she's pregnant! Can one night lead to parenthood *and* a lifetime of love?

LARGER-PRINT BOOKS!

GET 2 FREE LARGER-PRINT NOVELS PLUS
2 FREE GIFTS!

HARLEQUIN®

Romance

From the Heart, For the Heart

She stopped, close enough that she could almost feel his breath on her face, but still not touching. Violet looked up into his eyes and saw the control there. He was holding back. So she wouldn't.

Bringing one hand up to rest against his chest, she felt the thump of his heart through his shirt and knew she wanted to be close to that beat for as long as he'd let her. Slowly, she rose up onto her tiptoes, enjoying the fact that he was tall enough that she needed to. And then, without breaking eye contact for a moment, Violet kissed him.

It only took a moment before he responded, and Violet let herself relax into the kiss as his arms came up to hold her close. The celebrity wedding melted away, and all she knew was the feel of his body against hers and the taste of him on her lips. This. This was what she needed. Why had she denied herself this for so long?

And how could it be that kissing Tom somehow tasted like trust?

Eventually, though, she had to pull away. Tom's arms

kept her pressed against him, even as she dropped down to her normal height, looking up into his moss-green eyes.

"Is this where I give you some kind of line about getting to know me even better?" Tom asked, one eyebrow raised.

Violet's laugh bubbled up inside her, as if kissing Tom had released all the joy she'd kept buried deep down. "I think it probably is, yes."

"In that case, how long do you think we need to stay at this party?"

"There's five hundred people here," Violet pointed out. "What are the chances of them missing just two?"

"Good point." And with a warm smile spreading across his face, Tom grabbed Violet's hand and they ran for the waiting car.

Don't miss this enchanting conclusion to the
SUMMER WEDDINGS *trilogy,*
FALLING FOR THE BRIDESMAID.
Available June 2015 wherever
Harlequin® Romance books and ebooks are sold.

www.Harlequin.com

HREXP0515